The tangy scent of masculine aftershave teased Amie's nose.

Was it wafting from behind her? Or just clinging to her body to remind her of what she'd done?

Her grandmother took Amie's hand in a cool grasp. Despite her frailty, Mariah's grip was firm, confident. "Amie, dear, I was just looking for you to introduce you. But I see you and Preston have met."

Foreboding iced out residual passion. "Preston?"

Amie's brain worked overtime to make the pieces fit any other way but the one she feared.

Yet the magnetic, compelling man she'd just given herself to in a coat closet stepped around her, his eyebrows now pinched together as he whispered, "Amie?"

Her stomach dropped like she'd just fallen down an elevator shaft. Dawning realization robbed her of speech, her mouth bone-dry.

Her grandmother squeezed Amie's hand as she smiled at Preston.

"I'm so glad you've had a chance to get to know our new CEO."

* * *

Pregnant by the Cowboy CEO
is part of the Diamonds in the Rough trilogy: The McNair cousins must pass their grandmother's tests to inherit their fortune—and find true love!

Dear Reader,

My family is so precious to me. And as my children get married and my family expands, my heart just keeps growing bigger! When my husband and I started out on our journey to have a large family, we had great plans and hopes. But I had no idea the joy that awaited us. I also had no idea how much work goes into making those dreams come to fruition. Families are built, relationships worked on, differences valued. It truly is a journey, one to be treasured every step of the way.

That's a part of what I love so very much about writing family saga stories. Thank you so much for picking up book three in the Diamonds in the Rough series, following the McNair family through their journey. If you missed the first two books, they are still available: *One Good Cowboy* and *Pursued by the Rich Rancher*.

Happy reading!

Cathy

Catherine Mann

catherinemann.com

PREGNANT BY THE COWBOY CEO

CATHERINE MANN

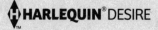

Recycling programs
for this product may
not exist in your area.

ISBN-13: 978-0-373-73398-9

Pregnant by the Cowboy CEO

Copyright © 2015 by Catherine Mann

This edition published by arrangement with Harlequin Books S.A.

For questions and comments about the quality of this book, please contact us at CustomerService@Harlequin.com.

Printed in U.S.A.

USA TODAY bestselling author **Catherine Mann** lives on a sunny Florida beach with her flyboy husband and their four children. With more than forty books in print in over twenty countries, she has also celebrated wins for both a RITA® Award and a Booksellers' Best Award. Catherine enjoys chatting with readers online—thanks to the wonders of the internet, which allows her to network with her laptop by the water! Contact Catherine through her website, catherinemann.com, find her on Facebook and Twitter (@CatherineMann1), or reach her by snail mail at PO Box 6065, Navarre, FL 32566.

Books by Catherine Mann

HARLEQUIN DESIRE

Diamonds in the Rough

One Good Cowboy
Pursued by the Rich Rancher
Pregnant by the Cowboy CEO

The Alpha Brotherhood

An Inconvenient Affair
All or Nothing
Playing for Keeps
Yuletide Baby Surprise
For the Sake of Their Son

Texas Cattleman's Club: After the Storm

Sheltered by the Millionaire

Visit the Author Profile page at Harlequin.com, or catherinemann.com, for more titles.

To my family—my world

Prologue

Two months ago

Amie McNair had never considered a one-night stand. Until now.

A champagne fountain gurgled beside her as she stared across the ballroom full of partiers gathered to celebrate her cousin's engagement. The night had been fun so far, but too similar to so many other glittering events that she attended in her work. She'd been thinking up an excuse to leave soon so she could trade her silky dress for the comfort of cotton pajamas. The jeweled choker at her throat was a gorgeous piece, but the yellow diamond at the base of her throat felt heavy. Tight. Like a collar keeping her neck in check. She liked her longer, bohemian-style pendants.

Those mundane thoughts scattered when he entered the room.

The broad-shouldered man striding confidently through the arched entryway pulled the air from her lungs. The connection was instantaneous. She wasn't quite certain why, but she forgot all about a desire for cotton pj's or the need to tug off her necklace. Her nerve endings sat up and paid attention.

Sure, he was tall, dark and hunky. But her world was filled with commanding, powerful men—from the cowboys that worked on her family's Hidden Gem Hobby Ranch, to the executives who worked in the family's Diamonds in the Rough jewelry-design empire. This man certainly measured up, from his muscled chest in the custom-tailored tuxedo, to the black Stetson he swept from his head and passed to an attendant near the entrance.

Yes, a Stetson and a tux.

And a boldly handsome face, tanned, with a strong square jaw. A face that had been lived in. His coal-black hair had a sprinkling of silver at the temples. That hint of age shouted wisdom, resolve. *Experience.*

A shiver tingled through her, gathering in all the right places.

Yet, in spite of all that, she found herself drawn most to his eyes. Even from halfway across the ballroom she could see they were a mesmerizing mix of gold and green that shifted ever so slightly with the chandelier sparkling overhead. She'd worked with amber that color in her jewelry designs and the changeable nature of the hue fascinated her. His gaze swept over her, past, then back again.

Holding.

That shiver inside her turned into a full-fledged fire. Her hand trembled and she set aside her champagne glass, her body already drawn forward in an undeniable magnetic pull. The urge to find out more about him propelled her feet across the room in time with the live band playing a classic Patsy Cline love song. Amie walked beneath the oversize, multicolored paper lanterns that decorated the room, toward the mystery man as he angled past guests in tuxes and formal gowns.

Other women noticed him, too, some of them watching every bit as intently as she did. But his eyes stayed on her as he closed the gap one bold step at a time.

Who was he? She knew most of the guests but didn't recognize him. Still, enough people nodded in greeting to him for her to know he wasn't a party crasher.

His gaze stroked over her, his hazel eyes gliding along her body like whispery smoke, confirming the awareness was reciprocated. She let herself relish the feeling, because honest to God, the last year had drained her. The grief over her grandmother's cancer, over the impending loss of the most important person in her life was heavy. Too heavy. From tip to toe, she hurt over losing her grandmother and, knowing Gran's legacy, her company was in the process of being handed over to a new CEO. So much change. Not the way her family's business was meant to be handled.

But right now, for the first time since her grandmother had announced her terminal brain tumor, there was a distraction from that ache in her heart.

A compelling, fascinating distraction.

She stopped in front of him, only a few inches apart. The crowd was so thick around them, the hum of their conversation and the band's tune created a false bubble of privacy. He held his silence, just looking back at her with a furrowed brow. Nice to know she wasn't the only one baffled by this moment.

She certainly didn't believe in love at first sight, but she couldn't deny the chemistry, the intense attraction, the connection that felt like more than simple lust. She understood physical attraction but considered herself beyond those superficial types of relationships. After all, her mother had trotted her across pageant stage from toddler days. Hair teased. Makeup. Ruffled custom dresses and shiny tap shoes.

Amie had been judged on her appearance, her walk, her smile for longer than she could remember. She'd seen enough backstabbing beauties with a Mona Lisa smile to know that the true value of a person went much deeper than the surface. Even knowing that, she couldn't deny how much she wanted this man.

She meant to say hello or introduce herself or ask his name. Instead, she glanced at his hand. No wedding ring. No tan line. "Are you married?"

A dark eyebrow lifted in a brief flash of surprise.

"Are you?" His voice rumbled between them with a hint of twang.

Local? Not quite. But definitely from a nearby region. His voice tripped along her senses, a deep tone that shivered against her skin.

She shook her head. "I'm not married."

"Me neither," he answered simply, without touching her. "Are you seeing anyone?"

She liked that it mattered to him. That said something good about him. "No. Are you seeing anyone?"

"Only the woman in front of me."

Oh. Damn. He was good. A small smile teased the corners of his mouth.

She wasn't sure exactly who moved first, but somehow her hand was tucked in the crook of his arm and he led her to the dance floor where they moved silently, their bodies in tune, step for step, through a slower country-music classic. The thick clusters of bright paper lanterns made the room glow with a rainbow of colors.

She breathed in his scent, clean but spicy, too. Masculine. Heady. His touch warmed her where he touched her waist. Her hand.

How long had it been since she'd felt a man's hands on her?

The energy between them crackled like static along her skin. Each chord from the string band strummed her oversensitive senses. She breathed in and he breathed out. Their steps synced effortlessly, her body responding to the slightest movement of his, shadowing his steps as she fell deeper into the spell of his gaze.

The dance gave her rare moments of pleasure in a year of hellish hurt and worry. No wonder she'd been drawn to him. She needed this. And in the same way that she could follow his steps, her body anticipating his next move, she could tell that he needed this, too. It was in his eyes. In the way his hand spanned her waist.

A step and swirl later and they were in the hall, then tucked in the deserted coatroom.

Then in each other's arms.

The dim lighting cast the room in shadows as she arched up into his kiss, his arms strong around her, but loose enough she could leave if she wanted. But the last thing she wanted was to stop. Pleasure pulsed through her at the angling of his mouth over hers, the touch of his tongue to hers. The kiss went deeper, faster, spiraling out of control in the quiet of the coat closet—a seriously underutilized space since it was spring in Texas.

Still, someone could walk in, and while she wasn't an exhibitionist, the possibility of discovery added an edge to an already razor-sharp need. The muffled sounds of music and partiers wafted under the door. She pressed herself to the hard planes of his body.

His arms moved up and he cupped her face, looking at her with those intense hazel eyes. "I don't do this sort of thing, tuck into coat closets with a stranger."

She covered his mouth with her hand. "We don't need to make excuses we have no way of knowing are true. This moment just…is. I don't understand why. But we're here." She took a deep breath of courage and said, "Lock the door."

Without a word, his hand slid behind him and the lock clicked in the long closet. The simple sound unleashed her barely contained passion. She looped her arms around his neck and lost herself in the kiss again. In the feel and fantasy of this man.

Her breasts tingled and tightened into hard beads of achy need. She couldn't remember when she'd been this turned inside out. She was thirty-one years old, not nearly a virgin. But she was unable to resist the draw of this stranger. The hard length of his erection pressed against her stomach, a heavy pressure that burned right through the silky dress she wore.

She couldn't deny where this was headed or that she wanted this. Him. Now.

His mouth traveled down her neck, then along her collarbone. "Condom. In my wallet," he said, his hands grazing under her breasts. "I'll get it."

He started to ease back and she stopped him, gripping his lapels.

"Let me."

Slipping her hand into his tuxedo jacket, she let her fingers stroke across the muscled heat of his chest. This was a man, the very best kind, powerful in body and mind. She tugged his wallet from inside his jacket and considered for an instant looking for a name, ...but her thoughts were scattered by his hands over her hips, gathering her dress. She plucked out a condom packet and tossed his wallet to the floor.

His hands were back on her just as fast, roving, keeping the flame burning.

She unzipped his pants as he lifted her hem. Her gown bunched around her hips, he hitched her up onto the small corner table where the coat check would normally pass out tickets during colder months. The wood was cool against her legs and then she slid them up and around his waist as he pressed against her, into her, with a thick pressure that sent a moan rolling up her throat.

It wasn't an elegant coupling. Her need was frenzied and his matched hers. This was crazy and out of control. And perfect. She lost herself in the pleasure, her senses heightened until everything felt...more. The tangy scent of his aftershave swirled inside her with every breath. Music muffled from the other room serenaded them, syncing their bodies into the most fundamental of dances.

And then thoughts disintegrated, the pace speeding, rising, bliss swelling inside her until she bit her lip to hold back a cry of pleasure that would betray their hideaway at any moment. He skimmed down the shoulder of her dress, dipping his head to take her breast in his mouth. That warm, moist tug took away the last of her restraint. Her head falling back, she surrendered to the orgasm sparkling through her like the facets off a diamond. The hoarse low sound of his release as he thrust deeply one last time sent another shimmer through her, leaving her languid, replete.

Using a last whisper of energy, she lolled forward. Her head rested on his shoulder as she waited for her racing heart to slow. His hands glided up and down her spine, easing her back to her feet, holding her up.

He smoothed her dress into place again and pressed a kiss to her temple. "We should tal—"

She shook her head. "Please. Don't say anything." She tugged her capped sleeve back over her shoulder and skimmed along her hair, the French braid having stayed miraculously in place, right down to the jeweled flower pin she'd clipped to the end of the braid. "Let's go back out. Go to separate sides of the room. And when, or if, we meet…it will be for the first time. Let this be what it is."

A fantasy. A once-in-a-lifetime crazy encounter— and she didn't want to hear it was commonplace for him. Didn't want to think about what she'd just done. Not while her body still trembled with pleasure and her heartbeat pulsed an erratic rhythm.

She didn't wait for his answer.

Reaching behind her, she simply unlocked the door, tucking out and around. Her legs were less than steady as she made her way back to the ballroom, and the sound of his footsteps close behind her didn't help. Was he following her? Was he going to insist or make a scene?

A mix of anticipation and dread made her chest tight with nerves.

The cool blast of the air conditioner in the hall rushed over her heated skin, goose bumps rising along her arms. The band still played, having picked up the speed with vintage Johnny Cash.

And before she could clear her head, she realized her grandmother had blocked her path. Mariah McNair looked regal but frail as she clutched her cane.

The tangy scent of masculine aftershave teased Amie's nose. Was it wafting from him behind her? Or just clinging to her body to remind her of what she'd done?

Her grandmother gripped the cane in a hand bearing sparkling jeweled rings. One of them was an amethyst heart Amie had designed as a teenager. With her other hand, Mariah took hers in a cool grasp, her skin paper thin and covered with bruises from IVs. Despite her frailty, Mariah's grip was firm, confident. "Amie, dear, I was just looking for you to introduce you. But I see you and Preston have met."

Foreboding iced out residual passion. "Preston?"

Her brain worked overtime to make the pieces fit any other way but the one she feared.

Yet the magnetic, compelling man she'd just given herself to in a coat closet stepped around her, his eyebrows now pinched together as he whispered, "Amie?"

Her stomach dropped as if she'd just fallen down an elevator shaft. Dawning realization robbed her of speech, her mouth bone dry.

Her grandmother squeezed Amie's hand as she smiled at Preston.

"I'm so glad you've had a chance to get to know our new CEO." Mariah extended her hand to the man. "Welcome to the Hidden Gem Ranch."

One

Two Months Later

Preston Armstrong was not a fan of weddings. Not even when he'd been the groom. Since his divorce ten years ago, he was even less entertained by overpriced ceremonial gatherings. He considered himself a practical businessman. That mind-set had taken him from a poor childhood to the top of the corporate ladder.

So, attending a marriage ceremony and seeing Amie McNair front and center of attention as a bridesmaid took his irritation to a whole deeper level—even now at the reception. Especially given that she'd ignored him for the past two months.

And most especially since she looked sexy as hell in a peach-colored bridesmaid's dress. Weren't those gowns supposed to be ugly, hated by bridal attendants around the world? But then, beautiful Amie with her luscious curves and confidence could probably make a burlap sack look sexy as hell. She'd won all those beauty-pageant titles for a reason.

Although he thought she was more alluring now with her at-ease boho look than the old runway-glitz photos that still periodically showed up in the social pages. Even her signature-designed coral teardrop earrings and necklace held his attention. Particularly the way that pendant nestled between the swell of her breasts.

He tipped his aged bourbon back, the sounds of the reception wrapping around him as he put in his required appearance at the McNair wedding event. He glanced at his watch, figuring he had to put in another half hour before he could check out and head back to the office. It was quiet there at night. He got more work done.

If Amie would talk to him alone for five damn minutes, he could reassure her that the closet encounter would never have happened if he'd known who she was. From the horrified expression on her face when her grandmother introduced them, clearly Amie didn't want anything to do with him either.

Business and pleasure should be kept separate. Always.

He didn't have the time or patience for awkwardness. He was confident. In charge. But that had all changed the minute he'd looked across the social function and saw a woman who'd flipped his world upside down.

This whole wedding week had gone to a new level of uncomfortable, to say the least. Being around Amie at work, they could keep things professional, if tense. It wasn't easy with all those thoughts of their explosive encounter hammering through his memory, but he managed to keep his boardroom calm intact.

However, the parties this week reminded him too much of that night he'd met her at the newlyweds' engagement shindig.

He'd meant it when he'd told her that impulsive encounter wasn't the norm for him. While he wasn't a monk, impetuous sex with strangers had never been his style. He'd spent a large part of his adult life married and monogamous. Then after his divorce, affairs had been careful, sensual but civil, with no long-term expectations.

He had affairs. Not hookups. And he sure as hell didn't have anonymous sex with a woman more than a decade younger than him.

Until Amie. Nothing about her followed a familiar pattern for him.

Keeping his hands to himself today was an exercise in torture, just as at work. Hints of her sucker punched his libido. The soft scent of her perfume lingering in his office after a meeting. The heat of her as she stood near him in a crowded elevator. And the list went on since she worked in the same building, her role as a renowned gemologist crucial to some of the most popular Diamonds in the Rough jewelry lines.

Up on the small stage in the oversize barn, the country band returned from their break, taking their place again and picking up instruments. Although to call it a barn didn't do the space justice. The reception was being held at the McNairs' hobby ranch, Hidden Gem, so the place was high end rustic, just like the company jewels.

Gold chandeliers and puffs of white flowers dangled

from the rough-hewn rafters. Strings of lights criss-crossed the ceiling, creating a starlit-night atmosphere. Bouquets of baby's breath and roses tied with burlap bows on the tables made him recall his earlier thought about Amie classing up a burlap sack. The inside had been transformed into rustic elegance, with gold chairs and white tulle draped throughout.

At the entry table next to the leather guestbook, seating cards were tied to horseshoes that had the bride's and groom's names engraved along with the wedding date. A cowbell hung on a brass hook with a sign that stated, Ring for a Kiss.

Good God. He wanted out of here. He knocked back the rest of the bourbon.

Amie's cousin Stone McNair, the former CEO of Diamonds in the Rough, was the groom, and there was no doubt he believed in all this forever, happily-ever-after nonsense as he twirled his blonde bride around on the dance floor.

At least the ceremony in the chapel had been brief. One bridesmaid and one groomsman—Amie and her twin brother, Alex. Amie's dark brown hair was loose, in thick spiral curls that made him want to tug just to see what she would do.

To hell with standing around. He might as well confront the awkwardness. It wasn't as if she could run away from him here.

He set aside the cut-crystal glass and strode through the crowd, a who's who list of Texas rich and famous. Just like that night two months ago, he made his way to her, this time determined for closure rather than a start of something.

Getting her semi-alone here shouldn't be too tough.

The exclusive venue had plenty of dark corners arranged for privacy so guests could visit and catch up.

He stopped behind her, smiling over her shoulder at the mayor. "I'm sorry to interrupt, but Miss McNair promised me this dance."

Amie gasped, her mouth opening to protest. But Preston took her hand and pulled her onto the dance floor before she could speak. He hauled her out in front of the small chamber orchestra, moving quickly before the stunned expression could melt from her elegant face. Before a closed, frosty one took its place. He'd watched that transformation too often over the last eight weeks and it was time to put an end to it.

He slid an arm around her and drew her close, those dark brown curls brushing him. "You look lovely tonight. Especially for being stuck in a bridesmaid's dress."

"It would have been nice to be asked if I wanted to dance. What are you doing?"

"Dancing with the groom's cousin. A perfectly acceptable move, nothing to draw attention to us. Unless you cause a scene out here in front of your whole family, our business acquaintances and some mighty prominent politicians."

Which he definitely did not want her to do. Then, he would have to let her go. And he liked the feel of her in his arms again too much to have her walk away yet.

"Fine," she conceded, blue eyes predictably turning to ice as she spoke. "Let's dance for appearances. Gran's always saying it's good for the company if we show a unified front."

Oh, he had her here for more than appearances and business. He was going to find a way to get past her cold shoulder. He couldn't stop the attraction, and chances were slim to none that he would be able to act on it. But he could damn well do something to disperse the tension between them.

He hoped.

Preston sidestepped another couple and swept her to a less crowded corner of the dance floor, mindful of the security guards posted around the perimeter of the event. "It's quite a party tonight. Congratulations to your cousin and his bride on their nuptials."

If Stone hadn't given up his role as CEO of Diamonds in the Rough, Preston wouldn't have been here. And the job was damn important to him. His job was all he had after the crash and burn of his personal life.

She smiled tightly, her body stiff and unyielding in his arms. "We do have all the tools for a first-rate wedding at our disposal."

The bride's thirty-thousand-dollar tiara had been custom designed for the event; in fact, a delicately understated piece that Amie had worked on personally for weeks. The tiara alone had created industry buzz and media coverage alike, a key piece in the company's new bridal collection.

"Do you realize this is the first time we've spoken about anything other than business?" He respected her work ethic, and discovering that admirable trait about her made this all the more difficult. Unlike her father, she was more than a figurehead. Amie contributed immeasurably to the company, so Preston crossed her path. Often.

She angled closer and for an instant he thought maybe... his pulse sped. His gaze dropped to her mouth. To her lips, parted.

And then, too soon, her breath teased against his

neck as she whispered, "I just want to make it clear, we won't be heading for the coat closet tonight."

There was no mistaking her determination. Too bad her method for delivering the news had him ready to sweep her off her feet and back to the cabin he'd reserved on the property for the night.

"I'm quite clear on that after your big chill these past two months." His hand twitched against her waist, the memory of her satiny skin still burned in his memory. "I'm just glad to know you're finally willing to acknowledge it happened."

"Of course it happened," she hissed between pearly-white teeth. "I was very much there."

The brush of her body against his was sweet torture. "I remember well."

Shadows shifted through her sky blue eyes. "Did you know who I was that night?"

Her words slowed his feet, stunning him. He picked up the dance pace again and asked, "Is that what you've thought all this time? That I played you on purpose?"

"Forget I said anything." She pulled back. "It doesn't matter now."

He strengthened his hold. "Not that you would believe me regardless of what I say. Although it was more than clear you didn't know who I was, and if you had, that night wouldn't have happened." He touched her face lightly. "And that would have been a damn shame."

They stood so close, their mouths only a couple of inches apart. He remembered how good she tasted—and how complicated that had made things for them the past couple of months. Having an affair with her would be a bad idea, given he was her boss and she was the granddaughter of the major stockholder.

But God, he was tempted.

So was she. He could see it in her jewel-blue eyes and the way she swayed toward him an instant before she stepped back.

Grasping his wrists, she pulled his arms from her. "I'm not sure what spurred you to reminisce right now since you don't seem to be the type to get sentimental at weddings. But now is not the time or the place for this discussion."

His eyebrows rose in surprise. "You're willing to talk then? Later?"

She held up a hand. "Talk. Only. I mean that."

"Let's step outside—"

"No. Not here. Not tonight."

He reached for her, sensing already she was just putting him off again. "Amie, if this is another stall tactic—"

"We'll have our secretaries check our calendars and schedule a lunch next week. Okay? Is that specific enough for you? Now, I need to check on my grandmother." She spun away in a swirl of peach silk.

Standing in the middle of the dance floor, he watched her walk away, the sway of her hips and those million-dollar legs peeking through a slit in the dress. Stepping off the dance floor, he wondered what the hell he hoped to gain in a conversation with her. An affair, given their work connection, was a bad idea, but he wasn't in the market for anything long term. Not again.

He charged back to the bar for another bourbon on the rocks, ignoring a waiter's offering of the evening's signature beverage, a Mouton Rothschild favored by the couple. Tonight, bourbon would do just fine. Marriage hadn't worked out well for him. At all. Just ask his ex.

He was too absorbed with work, too much of a loner. After all, a boss couldn't party with his subordinates, which put a serious dent in any kind of social life. He wanted to say that's what had made him so susceptible to Amie that first night, but he knew it was more than that. He was a man of control. Calm. Yet, the second he'd seen Amie, he'd claimed her with that first look in an explosive chemistry that went beyond any he'd experienced before, even with his ex-wife.

No wonder his marriage had failed early on. He'd made a fortune and in the end it hadn't made a bit of difference when things mattered most.

Rather than subject their daughter to a divorce, he and his wife had tried to hold it together for their child. But theirs had become a marriage in name only. Eventually, his ex had found someone else. She'd told Preston her new love would at least be around, which was better for Leslie than an absentee father. He'd bought into that, feeling guilty as hell and incapable of giving his child what she needed.

He'd replayed that decision a million times over, wondering if he'd fought harder for his marriage, for his child, if life could have turned out differently. Guilt piled on top of more guilt.

His baby girl had flown out of control during her teen years. Drugs, alcohol, sex. He'd tried grounding her, taking away her car, her allowance. He'd planned to take a vacation week to spend time with her, let her pick the vacation spot. She'd turned him down.

He should have persisted. He'd thought about it. Then it was too late.

Leslie ran off with her boyfriend the day after graduation, seventeen years old, pregnant. She'd ignored all offers of help and advice, determined to put her parents and the lifestyle she hated behind her. She hadn't cared about wealth or private jets. Hadn't wanted her own driver or a massive home. She'd even snubbed a doctor's care.

She and her baby boy had died seven months into the pregnancy. Premature delivery. Something with the placenta presenting first. His daughter, Leslie, bled to death. The baby lived for two days before dying.

The Armstrong portfolio was worth billions and his daughter and grandson had died from lack of prenatal care because she hated him that much. So much, she wouldn't take a penny or the most basic advice from him.

Some days the senselessness of it made it nearly impossible to hold back the rage.

The pain.

His child. Gone.

His ex blamed him. Damn it all, but he blamed himself, too.

So he put one foot in front of the other and existed.

Until that moment he'd seen Amie McNair. What was it about her? He wasn't the type to fall for a pretty face. But she was more than that. Not that he'd known as much that night. He'd just looked into her eyes and he'd seen...

Something that scared the hell out of him. Something worth going back for.

A risk he couldn't take again.

Pushing her grandmother's wheelchair down the hall to the family quarters, Amie took comfort from the ever-present scent of oak and pine that permeated the main lodge at Hidden Gem Ranch. The family wing could be accessed privately from the outside, but tonight, she'd taken the easier path through the lobby, waving to the night desk clerk on duty.

Now, as they passed through double doors that required a pass code, Amie could still barely breathe after how close she'd come to kissing Preston right there on the dance floor in front of everyone. She did not need people gossiping about the two of them. Especially not now. Damn him for rattling her. She needed to keep a cool head for her grandmother's sake.

Amie had never been known for her restraint.

She'd been sorely tempted to steal one more passionate moment with him before the inevitable conversation he'd insisted on having. But then her stomach had started churning and she'd made the excuse about secretaries and calendars before bolting.

Throwing up on his shoes would have been the worst way to tell him their night in the coat closet had created a baby.

Somehow, in spite of the condom, she was undeniably pregnant. She hadn't been with anyone else in six months, so there was no question about the paternity. She needed to tell him soon and agree on a plan before she shared the news with her grandmother.

Amie glanced down at her grandmother's gray head, her body frail from cancer, her once-long hair now short, just beginning to grow back from the latest round of treatments and surgeries that had only delayed the inevitable. "You overextended yourself this week, Gran."

Amie backed into her grandmother's suite of rooms, a decorative set of cattle horns on the door, an old joke of Gran's from her days in the corporate boardroom when a competitor had called her bullheaded. Gran had proudly taken to displaying this set on the front of her chauffeur-driven vehicle. These days, they resided on her door, still a reminder of her strength.

"Of course I did." Gran reached back to pat Amie's fingers on the handle, hand trembling. "I would rather die a day or two earlier than miss making the most of my grandson's wedding festivities."

"Well, that's blunt." Amie maneuvered the chair along a Persian rug, past a long leather sofa, the fireplace roaring with a warm blaze despite the summer temperature outside. Her grandmother appreciated the ambience and didn't mind the extra warmth in her more frail condition.

"You're one to talk considering you are just like me, stubborn as hell."

"I'll take that as a compliment, thank you very much."

Gran would be happy about the baby, no question. But Amie worried about the future because there was no way the critically ill woman would live long enough to see her great-grandchild's face. Amie couldn't bear to add more concerns. Beyond making her final days peaceful, stress was also a danger to her already fragile health. Amie needed to get her life together and develop a plan regarding Preston's role in their child's life. In this much, at least, she could be like her grandmother. Strong. Driven.

Calculating.

As the wheelchair rolled to a stop, Mariah folded her hands in her lap again. The bedroom was at once familiar and alien with its soaring high ceilings in rustic woodwork, supported by exposed beams in a darker wood. A two-tiered cast-iron chandelier hung over the living area, casting a warm glow, with lights that looked like gently flickering candles. Two wingback chairs bracketed the stone fireplace where she'd shared secrets and hot chocolate with her grandmother. But now there were additions to the place—a wheeled hospital cart of medical supplies and a leather recliner where the night nurse usually kept watch.

No doubt, Gran's caregiver would report in as soon as Amie sent her a text.

"Can I help you get settled? Bring you anything before I call for the nurse?" She took out her phone but wanted to stay. Wanted to visit the way they used to, never caring how late the hour.

Her eyes burned as she blinked away unexpected tears.

Her grandmother gestured for her to sit. "Amie, I've lived a full life. Of course I would have liked to have more, or at the very least live these last days in full health. But I'm making the most of the time I have left. I've seen one grandson married and have hopes the other grandson will be settled soon."

Ouch. No mention of her granddaughter. Just that Stone was married, and Alex had found the perfect woman. She swallowed hard.

"Alex and Nina are happy, and her son, Cody, is precious." She was happy for Alex. Her twin's joy was her joy.

"It's good to see a child here in the house again. I've missed the laughter of a little one."

Did her grandmother know? Was she hinting for an admission or just referencing Cody? Shooting to her feet, she turned away to hide any telltale expressions on her face. Amie picked up the pewter pitcher on the bedside table and refilled her grandmother's water glass, unable to pull her eyes away from the photo of her grandparents on their wedding day. "You should turn in early and conserve your strength for the family breakfast tomorrow."

"I'm resting now and my strength isn't going to return," she said with a dry laugh. She sipped her water, cleared her throat and continued, "I don't have to sleep to relax. Let's talk."

"About what?" Her skin prickled. She sat on the chaise at the end of the four-poster bed that had been converted into a queen-size hospital bed. Unwilling to think about that—and how hard life had become for her beloved grandmother, Amie bent to breathe in the delicate scent of lilies of the valley in a big bunch on the nightstand.

Gran set aside her glass of water. "Stone and Alex have both passed their test to assure me they can handle their share of the inheritance, that they can carry on the McNair tradition in the spirit I would wish."

Her cousin Stone had surprised them all by stepping down as CEO of Diamonds in the Rough and developing his nearby land. He'd started an equine therapy camp for children with special needs. Her twin brother, Alex, had gained their grandmother's trust to keep running the Hidden Gem Ranch and opened up parts of the facility for Stone's camp.

"Ah, so now you get to the reason for this conversation." She sagged back, clutching a decorative pillow protectively. "What do you have cooked up for me?"

"You don't need to look so worried." A smile lighting her sapphire-blue eyes, Gran smoothed her grandmother-of-the-groom turquoise satin dress, the hem heavy with silver embroidery that mimicked a Diamonds in the Rough necklace she favored.

"Of course I'm worried. And more than a little curious. You saved my test for last for a reason, I'm sure.

I assume that's because my challenge is the most difficult. Or I'm the most difficult to deal with." A bitter
memory from her past seeped in. "Mom always cov-
eted that slot to perform last in a pageant to keep me
foremost in the judges' minds. After the bar had been
raised as high as possible, she figured I would know
how well I had to perform to win."

Like the year her mother had changed Amie's baton-
twirling act into a fire-throwing stunt—just half an
hour before Amie took the stage—since another girl
had done a great baton act. Amie would have never
guessed her mother could find a way to light the ends
of her batons on fire in thirty minutes. But with Mc-
Nair wealth and a helpful hotel concierge, anything was
possible for a demanding pageant mother. Amie hadn't
burned down the building or set herself on fire, but she
hadn't won and she'd been scared as hell.

Gran's smile faded and sympathy filled her eyes.
"The test I have in mind isn't like your mother making
you compete in all those beauty pageants."

"Isn't it?" Amie said bitterly, then felt guilty right
away. It wasn't her grandmother's fault. "Never mind.
Forget I said that. I know you're not like Bayleigh… You
love me, so whatever you're doing must be for a reason."

"Your mother loves you, dear, she's just…"

"Self-absorbed." There was no denying the truth.
"I've acknowledged that and moved on. I'm an adult
and I accept responsibility for my own feelings."

Gran tipped her head to the side. "You say that, but
until this moment, I never realized this test would make
you feel as if my love is conditional…like your mother's."

"Does that mean I'm off the hook with my challenge?

You'll fire Preston and put me in charge?" she asked, only half joking.

"Oh dear, you always did have a great sense of humor," Gran said affectionately. "This isn't about my love for you. Love isn't about money. You have millions with your trust fund and personal earnings. This is about figuring out where you best fit professionally in the business."

"What if I do like Stone and decide to build my own future?" She just wished there was something else she wanted to do, but she lived and breathed to work at Diamonds in the Rough.

Or at least she had until Preston showed up and took away the job she'd hoped for as her own.

"That's your choice. But keep in mind Stone still took his test because he knew that would put my mind at ease. These requests of mine are because I love you and I want the best for you."

Amie sighed, exhaustion stealing through her. "I do know that, Gran."

Her grandmother's shoulders braced. "This week Preston Armstrong is traveling in support of the unveiling of our new line. I want you to go with him."

She waited for the rest and...nothing. "That's it?" Amie asked, incredulous. "That's my test?"

"Yes, be civil. Don't cause a scene. Truly show the world that we're a unified force, even away from the office, and stockholders will be reassured."

"A week on the road with no scenes." She'd kept her distance from him for two months, she could do so for longer.

"That's all."

"You're letting me off rather easy," she conceded,

hoping she could finish up some design work on the trip since she'd been working night and day on a secret collection—a labor of love that she worried wasn't right for Diamonds in the Rough.

"I don't think so." Her grandmother shook her head. "Not considering the cold shoulder you've given him these past couple of months."

She could have sworn she'd kept that from her grandmother. Mariah wasn't at the office often at all. Amie had imagined—hoped—her chilly reception would be perceived as businesslike.

She'd guessed wrong. "I apologize if you think I haven't been receptive to your new CEO. I thought I was simply being professional."

"Don't try that innocent act with me," Gran snorted. "You won't even stay in the same room with him unless forced by a meeting. I'm not sure what your differences are and I don't need to know. We are very lucky to have lured him away from his job in Oklahoma. It was a big sell convincing him this job would increase his corporate appeal as a man of serious net worth and business importance. I do not want to lose him at Diamonds in the Rough, as our stocks continue to rise since we announced he was taking the helm."

"Rising at the expense of firing some of our most loyal, long-serving middle management," she reminded her grandmother.

"And I can see you're still bitter about that decision to consolidate here and expand other offices."

Amie pressed her lips together to keep from arguing with her grandmother, something that would only stress her out since clearly this battle was already lost.

Gran nodded wearily. "Reconcile with him. Because,

like it or not, he is the CEO, and if having you there up-sets the flow of business, well, I can't have that."

The full weight of her grandmother's words sunk in. "Are you threatening to fire me?"

And just as troubling, what did Preston have to do with this? Had he been pressuring Gran to nudge her out of the company? Or to find another angle to wran-gle his way into her bed?

His approach tonight might not have been coinci-dental. He could have set this whole thing up, damn him. Anger fired hotter inside her, almost a welcome relief after the frustrated passion, fear for her child—and grief for Gran.

"Let's not borrow trouble. Focus on the week and learn to forge a friendship with Preston."

Friendship? With the father of her child from a one-night stand? And how was he going to react to the news of the baby? Gran's request might not even be possible. "What if Preston doesn't agree? Or if he's antagonistic?"

Her grandmother smiled with a narrow-eyed deter-mination Amie recognized well. "Then you'll just have to win him over. Because, like it or not, your days of avoiding him are done."

Two

Hands jammed in his tuxedo pockets, Preston strode away from the barn to the resort cabin where he planned to spend the night. Most of the guests were either staying in the main lodge or in one of the bungalows scattered around the property.

He'd done his duty at the reception, put in an appearance. With luck, he could pull out his laptop and log some extra hours preparing for his upcoming business trip. He would try to numb his mind and body against the attraction. Just being near Amie at the wedding had desire pumping through him. He needed to come up with some kind of plan to work with her without this eating them both alive, but damned if he knew which way to turn. For now, burying himself in reports and numbers would have to do.

The reception was still going strong in the towering barn, music and conversation swelling out into the night. The lodge itself held two wings, one for family suites and the other for guests. Then the cabins offered larger, more private space, farther away from the din of the ongoing party.

A movement from the family quarters snagged his attention, a shadowy figure charging across a first-floor veranda. The moonlight cast a glow, illuminating the unmistakable silhouette of... Amie. She paused at the railing, scanning the grounds. She was looking for him—that was clear the second her gaze landed on him.

Her shoulders went back, her breasts straining at the strapless dress, teardrop earrings brushing her bare shoulders. She flicked her long hair over her shoulder, her eyes narrowing. She stomped down the porch steps, hem of her bridesmaid's gown in her fists and hitched to her knees so she could storm closer all the faster. Something had lit her fuse. He wanted her attention back on him anyway.

He stopped in his tracks and waited. Anticipation pumped through him. Even mad, she was incredible, a sight not to be missed. Besides, there was something about knowing he got under her skin this much. That he'd put all that spark and fire inside her.

She stopped in front of him under the shade of a sprawling oak strung with white lights. Her breasts rose and fell rapidly, enticingly. "Are you responsible for this?"

Responsible for what? He could hardly think with her so close, her heaving breasts nearly brushing his chest. He would only need to move one step closer. "You'll need to narrow that down for me."

"You said on the dance floor that we need to talk soon." She jabbed him in the chest with one finger.

He grabbed her finger. "And you said our secretaries need to set up a lunch next week."

"Did you know that couldn't possibly happen? Did you pressure my grandmother into making me travel with you around the country this week?"

He dropped her hand. He didn't know what the hell she was talking about. He was heading out for a week to launch a new line for Diamonds in the Rough, but he'd made no plans to take her along. Apparently she thought otherwise for some reason.

Still, that didn't explain her angry reaction. They'd worked together for two months. Why was she so upset about this trip? He was missing something and he wasn't sure what.

But he intended to find out. "Why would I go out of my way to insist on that?"

"For a week of repeats of our encounter in the coat closet two months ago."

Righteous indignation steamed through him. "Have I pressured you in any way that would make you assume that I would disregard your wishes? Because I take the issue of sexual harassment in the workplace damn seriously."

"No, you haven't done anything inappropriate," she acquiesced, chewing her full bottom lip. "But you sounded determined tonight. I just had to know if you're manipulating me behind the scenes as well."

Unable to resist taunting her, he stepped closer, letting his gaze linger on her mouth as their bodies brushed. "Should I have?"

A light flashed in the night sky and an appreciative

murmur went up from a crowd gathered on the western lawn. The fireworks show had started to celebrate the nuptials.

"Quit twisting my words around." She tipped her face toward him without backing down, her creamy skin lit by the purple-and-white lights sparking overhead. "I don't like being played, that's all."

He swept a stray lock of silky dark hair over her shoulder, his knuckles skimming her soft skin, the teardrop earring cool across the top of his hand. "I take this to mean we're going on a business trip together this week."

The crowd watching fireworks cheered as a series of pops and bangs ended in a giant red heart burning into the cloudless Texas sky.

Her eyebrows pinched together, her gaze never wavering to watch the display. "You really don't know about my grandmother's plan for us?"

Gently, he gripped her shoulders and turned her so she could see the bright red heart before it faded. While she watched, he leaned closer to speak into her ear.

"I have no reason to lie to you." In fact, he just wanted to open a dialogue with her so they could figure out how to work together—or resume the affair. He couldn't help but wonder if part of the reason they kept sparking off each other was that they hadn't let all that attraction run its course. "It's been tough breaking through your walls these past two months, but I wouldn't go to someone else to take care of that problem for me. And I certainly wouldn't worry a terminally ill person with my concerns."

She turned to face him again, giving him a clipped nod, some of the tension easing from her while the orchestra played a Mozart piece timed to coordinate with the explosions in the air.

He leaned back against the tree trunk and jammed his hands into his pockets and away from temptation. "Now catch me up to speed about what's going on with this business trip, since it appears to involve us both and Diamonds in the Rough."

"My grandmother has insisted that I accompany you for the unveiling of the new line to reassure the stockholders that the McNairs fully endorse your leadership." Sighing, she perched a hand on her hip.

Preston's gaze fell to her waist, the dips and curves of her so damn alluring his mouth watered. "That's a sound business decision on her part. What's the problem?"

He didn't understand why she was so upset. She'd worked hard on the new line, had invested a lot of time and creative energy toward putting it together. She deserved to see the first public reactions to her work.

But she shook her head. Visibly upset.

"The problem is… She's an amazing woman and I just want to do what she needs." She blinked back tears, making her blue eyes shine in the reflected light from the soaring roman candles in a multicolored display. That sheen in her gaze made him want to hold her.

"Amie?" He resisted the urge to reach for her, half certain she would bolt. "Losing someone you love is not easy. I'm sorry about your grandmother's illness."

"Me, too." She swiped her wrist over her eyes, smudging mascara. "So we're traveling together this week for the unveiling tour. Just the two of us."

"Apparently so." He wondered what her grandmother was up to with this last-minute idea and why she hadn't discussed it with him first. "To Los Angeles, New York City and Atlanta. It may be for the best. We have to figure out how to work together without all this tension."

He had sensed that Amie was working on a private project these last few weeks and he wondered why she hadn't shared any details. That kind of closed-off creativity didn't benefit the larger company. He needed her communicating more.

Had that been Mariah McNair's intent, to smooth the business waters before she passed away? It wasn't such an odd wish. The woman did live, eat and breathe the business, even from her sickbed.

Amie crossed her arms over her chest, her breasts pushing even harder against the fabric. "We've been doing fine so far at the office."

"Are you serious?" These had been some of the most tense workweeks in his life. He'd never had personnel problems—until now. Until her.

"Has my work performance been in any way substandard?"

"Of course not," he admitted, not mentioning the way she'd retreated to her office for long periods at a time with her door closed. "But it would help workplace morale if you didn't act like you want me dead."

Her shoulders sagged, her eyes softening. "I do not want you dead."

"Then how exactly do you want me?" He stepped closer, his eyes falling to her mouth, to her full lips. Amie McNair had a way of knocking the props out from under him by just walking into a room, and he was damn tired of tap dancing around the subject. He was too old for games.

The fireworks on the lawn churned faster, shot after

shot popping and exploding, sending showers of sparks into the night sky. The fireworks reflected in Amie's eyes as she stepped back, expression iced over again. "If we're going to be away for a week, I should start packing."

Turning, she marched across the grass, her beautiful body illuminated by white lights in the sky that turned on and off, on and off.

Just like Amie herself.

Amie was exhausted to her toes. Not just from the wedding but from the shocking talk with her grandmother to the confrontation with Preston.

She was truly going to spend a week alone with him.

Closing her bedroom door, she finally let her guard down. Kneeling, she held out her hands for her cats, a gray tabby in her lap, a Siamese at her feet, both hers, and Mariah's two Persians as well. Yes, she was just shy of a crazy-cat-lady starter kit, but her furbabies brought her comfort. With a final stroke along each feline's arched back, she stood. She'd loved growing up on a farm with animals all around, even if her room was far from rustic, a jewel box of a space, from the strands of multicolored glass beads around her bed, to the stained-glass insets in the high windows above her reading area.

Walking out of her shoes, she reached behind her to unzip the bridesmaid's dress. She shimmied it down and kicked it aside. She sagged to sit on the edge of her bed. She flopped back on the bed, the silk of her camisole and tap pants soft against her skin still tingling from Preston's touch. Damn it, she hated losing her composure. And to lose it twice in one night?

Her hand slid over her stomach. No baby bump yet, but soon more than just her breasts would be swelling. And her hormones were out of control, leaving her tearful most of the time and nauseated the rest of the time. Her figure would soon be evident to everyone. No more pageant jokes about her size.

She'd been the first runner-up in the Miss Texas pageant over a decade ago, reportedly the first beauty competition she'd lost since her mother had teased up her hair and sent Amie tap-dancing out on the stage at four years old. She'd "Good Ship Lollipopped" her way through puberty into bikinis and spray tans. Her mama had lived for her daughter's wins.

She didn't even want to think about her parents' reaction to her pregnancy.

There wasn't anything she could do about it tonight and she truly was exhausted. No matter how much she slept, her body demanded more. She reached on the bedside table for her mouth guard by the phone. Tension had made her grind her teeth at night since she was seventeen and entered higher-stakes pageants.

She'd already seen a doctor to confirm and start prenatal vitamins. The appointment had been scary and exciting at the same time. Preston deserved the opportunity to be a part of his child's life from the start—if he wanted. She would have to tell him about the baby this week. It wasn't fair to wait any longer. This was his child too. She would just have to find the right time. His reaction would also have a lot to do with how she presented the news to the rest of her family.

If only she knew him better, knew how he would react, how he would want to proceed. She was capable and prepared to take care of the baby herself. But she didn't want her child to live with a father's rejection.

She squeezed her eyes shut and buried her face in her pillow, wishing she could will herself to sleep faster.

The phone rang on her bedside table, jarring her. Was something wrong with her grandmother?

Flinging back the covers, she grabbed the receiver and pulled out her mouth guard. "Hello?"

"Amie?" her twin brother's voice filled her ear. "Are you okay?"

"Of course." She tugged the covers back up again. "Why do you ask?"

"You left the reception before it was over. That isn't like you."

They always had been in tune with each other's moods. Her brother wasn't normally a chatty person, so for him to call, he must sense something was up. But she wasn't ready to tell him. It wouldn't be fair to tell anyone before Preston.

"Gran was tired, so I took her back to her room, then I decided to slip out. I did see the fireworks display though. It was a beautiful touch." No way was she telling him about Gran's test. He would worry, wonder— question. "I hope you don't mind that I left the hosting duties to you."

"Of course I don't mind. We're family. You've been carrying more than your fair share of the McNair face time for Hidden Gem business this past year. The reception was winding down by the time you left. Mother and Father were in their element entertaining anyway."

"They do like to play the head-of-the-family role."

Their parents lived off a trust fund, tightly managed by Gran's lawyers. Their cousin Stone's mother also lived off her trust fund, working to stay clean after multiple stints in drug rehab. Leaving the bulk of her estate to her grandchildren was a huge vote of confidence from Gran that Amie didn't take lightly. Her grandmother's respect meant everything to her.

Amie was determined to do better by her own child than her stage mom, Bayleigh. Without question, Mariah was the better role model.

Amie tucked the phone more securely under her neck. "Was there anything else?"

"What was up with you and Armstrong on the dance floor? Any progress getting along better with the new boss? He's really not such a bad guy. We had a good time playing cards at the bachelor party."

"Have you been talking to Gran?" she asked suspiciously.

"No, I just got to know him better with all the wedding parties this week. We talked some."

"Talked about what?"

He laughed softly. "You sound nervous."

The twin bond was sure a pain in the butt sometimes. "I'm not nervous. I'm just exhausted." Really exhausted. She'd never been as tired in her life as she'd been the past few weeks. "Good night, Alex. Love you." She hung up the phone and resisted the urge to pull the covers over her head.

Someone was going to guess soon and her secret would be out. She needed to control the telling.

Sunday morning, Preston waited beside the limo, outside the Hidden Gem Ranch. It wasn't like Amie to be late. Ever. She was always one of the first at work and last to leave. But she'd kept him out here hanging around for over twenty minutes.

He definitely wasn't accustomed to anyone making him wait. Maybe she was playing a mind game?

The door to her quarters opened and she backed out onto the veranda, her curvy bottom wriggling as she juggled her purse and some kind of bag. Turning, she faced him and started forward, wearing turquoise high heels, pencil jeans and a flowy white shirt with multiple strands of signature McNair necklaces. The long loops of her necklaces drew his eyes down her body, hinting at the curves that lay beneath the shirt.

As always, he braced for the fact she damn near took his breath away.

His eyes fell to the little pink leopard-print carrier that wobbled back and forth to the side as something fuzzy and shadowy moved around inside. He frowned. "I thought you said you were packing clothes? Not livestock."

Stopping in front of him, she lifted up the frilly carrier. "Clearly this isn't large enough for a horse. I sent my bags ahead to the airport. This is one of my carry-ons. It may come as a surprise to you, but I do not travel light."

He opened the limo door for her. "You're one of those types that takes a cute little dog everywhere."

"Don't let my cat hear you call him a dog. He hates that." She slid into the long leather seat.

"You travel with a *cat*?" He dropped into the seat across from her and stared at the carrier beside her. This woman never failed to surprise him in every way possible.

"Are you saying cats miss their humans less than dogs?"

"No—" he chose his words carefully "—cats are more independent. More easily left on their own."

"Well, I won't be leaving this one." Her chin tipped. "If you have a problem with that, you can be the one to call off the trip." She flashed a thin smile at him. "Could you possibly be allergic?"

Was that her plan? To get him to bail? It would take a lot more than a feline to make that happen. Still, he couldn't help digging. "I am not allergic to cats—or dogs, for that matter. But surely someone on the staff can handle that. You have other pets."

"This one is special." She unzipped the top and the fluffy Siamese's head popped out. The cat yawned and stared at Preston with blue eyes just as intense as Amie's. "He's old and has diabetes. He needs his injections."

Guilt kinked his neck. "I'm sorry for leaping to conclusions." He shook his head. "But I have to confess, I still don't get it. You have the money for fancy pet sitting, including injections. So you need his company? Don't you have two or three other or a dozen other cats? There are varying accounts around the office of how many. How did you pick which one to bring?"

"Four. Just four," she said tightly. "My other three cats are staying with Gran. But I only trust Johanna with this one since she's a vet tech, and as you know, she is on her honeymoon. Other than her, there's no one I trust to administer the medication who's also familiar to Roscoe—"

"Roscoe? I thought your family named all people and animals after gems." Her brother was actually Alexandrite and she was Amethyst. Even their horses had gemstone names.

"My grandmother and my parents did that with the names. I don't. Trust me, learning to write Amethyst in preschool wasn't easy. So, this is Roscoe. It fits." She smoothed a hand over his head. "I know I could hire some high-end pet sitter for him, but his diabetes gets worse when he's stressed, and when he misses me, he stresses."

"We can't have that happening." He scratched a furry ear and the cat erupted into a low, humming purr.

"This is not a joke," she snapped, hugging the carrier closer. "I couldn't bear it if he passed away while I was gone. I'm important to him and he's important to me."

He rested his hand on her knee. "I'm not laughing at you. I'm just wondering if the cat is going to need jewelry for the galas too."

"Ha-ha. I'm not taking him to work with me." Her gaze flicked to his hand and she chewed her bottom lip. "Just traveling and keeping him in my suite."

"You genuinely seem to care." And that made her all the more attractive somehow.

"I do." She lifted his hand from her knee, but the flush on her neck showed she wasn't unaffected. "Now, can we get going? The plane is waiting."

He let the air crackle between them for an instant before signaling the driver. It was going to be an interesting—and tempting—week.

Three

Amie buckled her cat's carrier into the seat beside her on the luxury jet, larger than the McNair family's plane, with more space for the lengthy travel planned for the week. Plush leather seats. A semicircular sofa around a dining table, with a galley kitchen off to the side. Even a small shower and sleeping area curtained off.

Other than a pilot behind the bulkhead wall, she was alone with Preston for all of the flights. Day and night. She sagged back in the leather recliner, the sounds of Preston across the row tempting her to look. Just sitting in the limo with him had been tempting. That's why she had strengthened her defenses. She had to. What would this week—even the past two months—have been like if she wasn't pregnant? Would she have eventually fallen under the spell of the sexy, brooding CEO in spite of the fact he ran the company she'd once hoped to head?

Unlikely once the pink slips had started being handed out to employees. Sure, he was getting results, but she still wasn't convinced his way was the best way. Maybe she could use this week to find out his future plans for the company. And if they involved more of his hatchet style of leadership? She hoped to persuade him to find a compromise that didn't gut the heart of the family business.

She jammed earbuds in to prevent further conversation and closed her eyes against the morning nausea. She *felt* Preston settle in his seat. Instinctively, she reached for the volume control, pressed the button and tried to lose herself in the music. Anything to dull her interest in the man sitting across from her. She kept her eyes shut, and tried her best to relax her jaw. To be natural and unconcerned even though her nerves were raw.

This was really happening. She'd wondered how she would tell him about the baby and now it was clear that conversation would have to happen this week. At the end of their travels, because if she told him sooner, the rest of the trip would be impossible to withstand. She had to use this time to find common ground, a peace of sorts before telling the rest of the family.

Easier said than done.

He was an arrogant man. A fair boss, but distant. Cool. She wanted and needed more in her life. She'd been left with no choice in her distant parents. But she'd seen her grandparents' marriage and the way they loved their family unconditionally. She would settle for nothing less for herself or her child.

The plane taxied and took off smoothly. Amie thought she might just get away with listening to her favorite folk music all the way until lunch. And if he lost himself in work, maybe she could pull out some of her own sketches for the collection she hadn't shared with anyone else. Ideas were buzzing in her head for the snake-themed coils she'd designed, the patterns of their markings inspiring interlocking pieces for multicolored chains in precious metal. They were more urban and sophisticated than the rustic luxury items that were the company cornerstone, potential crossover items into a younger, more international market while staying true to her roots.

She hadn't shared them because what if they ventured too far off the mark? Weren't as good as she hoped? She didn't think she'd get sacked for stepping outside the design aesthetic, although with Preston at the helm...who knew? Her bigger concern was that she'd spent time designing pieces that would never be made. The artist in her mourned that.

Then she felt a gentle tug on an earbud. A sideways glance revealed Preston with the earpiece dangling between his fingers.

His face was open, receptive. "Now that we're settled for the trip, do you want to tell me why you've gone out of your way to ignore me since that night in the coat closet?"

Leave it to a man—and a billionaire CEO at that—to be direct.

"We work together. It isn't wise to pursue a personal relationship." The sight of him in a black suit and leather cowboy boots threatened to take her breath away even now. She had continued to want him over the past two months. That was part of the problem.

All that male arrogance and remorseless reorganization hadn't done nearly enough to make her body stop wanting him.

"Amie, clearly we have to find a less antagonistic way to be in the same room." He draped the earbud over her armrest, just a hairsbreadth away from her arm. "I assume that's why your grandmother sent us on this outing, to keep drama out of the workplace."

"Drama?" She plucked the other earbud out and resisted the urge to toss something at his head. "Are you calling me a drama queen? I am a professional in every way at the office. You're the one who thinks I'm plotting your death."

"Okay, we've agreed you don't want to tie concrete blocks to my ankles and throw me in the Trinity River, but you're still a professional dripping ice every time I walk into the room." He leaned on his armrest, coming closer and pinning her with a laser gaze. "I wouldn't put up with this from any employee, male or female, no matter who they're related to. I find nepotism to be abhorrent, in fact."

Nepotism? The word seared her. She worked twice as hard as anyone else to prove otherwise and still she couldn't catch a break. If she didn't love the family company so much, she would have left long ago. "I apologize if I've been less than cordial or in any way taken advantage of my family connections."

"There's that ice I was talking about. Combined with a beauty pageant answer—carefully worded."

She smiled tightly, irritated and turned on—and scared. "Well, you're the one asking for world peace."

"Just a cease-fire."

"I want that, too." She needed it. For their child's sake. "I'm just not sure how. This probably sounds strange after what we did two months ago, but I really don't know you."

The steel in his gaze lightened. He leaned back in his chair, hands crossed over his chest. "Ask me anything you want to know."

"Anything?" *How would you feel about becoming a daddy in seven months?* Probably not wise to lead with that one.

"Sure," he said. "On one condition."

Damn. She'd known this supposed cease-fire was too good to be true. "I am not sleeping with you again just to find out your favorite color."

"I didn't ask you to," he pointed out. "My condition is simple. For every question you ask, I get to ask one as well. You can even choose who goes first."

Sounded fair, and as he'd mentioned, all those pageants sure had given her a wealth of practice in dodging sticky questions. "All right, why did you take this job when you were making more money at the sportswear corporation in Oklahoma?"

"Your grandmother is quite persuasive. I don't need the money. But I do need a challenge."

"Is that what I am to you? A challenge?"

He smiled, hazel eyes glinting. "That's another question when I haven't asked you anything."

"All right, your turn." She sighed warily, her tummy flipping with nerves and a hint more morning sickness. "Ask away."

"What's your favorite color?"

She blinked fast, waiting for the other shoe to drop. "Seriously? That's it?"

"Do you want a tougher question? Something more personal? Because I can think of more than one of that sort."

"Fuchsia," she blurted. "My favorite color is fuchsia. What's yours?"

"Don't care."

"Then why ask me my favorite?" She couldn't help but wonder.

"I've found I can tell a lot about a person by their choice. I catalogue those picks, like crayons in a box, and track the trends. It's like analyzing data in the workplace."

"Wait. Seriously?" She held up a hand as something else occurred to her. "You're working for a jewelry empire and you don't care about the nuances of beauty in jewel tones? Just an overall trend of some Crayola personality test?"

"I care about tracking sales data. I'm not a designer. I have people for that. A good boss knows who to promote based on job performance—not bloodlines." He hinted at that distrust of nepotism again. "What made you choose to stay in the family business rather than strike out on your own?"

She searched for the right words to explain something innate. "It's in my blood, all I can ever remember wanting to do. In fact, my earliest memories are of accompanying my grandfather to work."

"What did you do at the company as a toddler?"

"You'll have to wait. It's my turn to ask. Based on all that cataloguing of favorite color trends, what do you think would be your favorite color—if you ever decided to choose one?"

"What?" He looked at her as if he was dizzy from following her through a maze.

"What type of person are you? If I'm fuchsia, what are you?"

"Um, navy blue, maybe dark gray."

Why did she want to know? "You didn't think about that, did you? I believe you just made up an answer."

"Prove it," he said smugly, crossing his arms over his chest. Even through the black shirt, she could see the outline of muscles in his arm. His smile was genuine, if not a little playful, and his eyebrow cocked with such arrogance that she couldn't look away.

She scrunched her nose. "You're not playing fair with this question game."

He leaned forward again, closer this time. "I don't know the answer to your color question and I really want to get to my question. What did you do with your grandfather at work?"

She found herself drawn in by the timbre of his voice as much as the steel in his eyes. "He asked me to help him make a necklace for Gran's birthday. Picking out the stones. Choosing which of his designs I liked the best. It was…magical."

"Your grandparents are important to you." He was a perceptive man.

She needed to remember that.

"My grandmother is the primary reason I'm here. She and Gramps were more parents to me than my own—which is no great secret to anyone who's been around for any length of time. I hate that I'm missing even a day with her on this trip, but this is what she wants."

"If making your grandmother happy is that important, that brings me back to my first question. Why have you been avoiding me?"

There was no more hiding the truth from him or herself.

"I'm not sure how to be in the same room with you without thinking about the day we met."

Amie's admission still rattled around in Preston's brain even hours later after they'd checked into their Los Angeles hotel on California's renowned Gold Coast. He paced around the sitting area between their rooms, picture windows overlooking the water. Crystal, brass and high-end upholstery filled the place. He wasn't much on décor, but he knew "good" when he was around it. He hadn't grown up with this kind of luxury, but he'd grown accustomed to it over the years climbing the corporate ladder.

A knock sounded at the door. "Room service."

Preston went to admit the catering staff, allowing them to set up the wet bar with a tray of fruit and vegetables, plus a selection of finger sandwiches and teas. He'd asked what a light lunch would be for a woman and he had to admit the spread looked good. There would be food at the gala tonight, but he thought Amie might like something ahead of time.

Tipping the servers, he went to Amie's door and knocked.

"Amie?" The door nudged open. It must not have been latched in the first place.

A silver ball of fur streaked past his feet.

"Roscoe!" Amie streaked just as fast, wearing a T-shirt and cotton shorts that were…short. He probably shouldn't have noticed that when she was chasing her escapee cat.

But her hair was in a topknot on her head. No jewelry anywhere. And she had a down-to-earth appeal that kicked him square in the chest. It took him a minute to move past that and notice that she sidestepped a baby grand piano and one-of-a-kind furnishings like a shifty running back, finally pouncing on Roscoe before he slipped into Preston's room.

"Those were some moves," he drawled, trying hard to lift his eyes from the sight of her bare thighs.

"I might not have had to move so fast if I'd had a little help." She arched an eyebrow at him, no trace of makeup on features that didn't need it.

"I was…distracted." He couldn't help a slow grin at her glare. "I'll help now though. Do you need his carrier?"

He peered inside her bedroom and noticed a spread of papers on her bed. Sketches of jewelry designs that she'd inked in with bright, bold colors in snakeskin patterns.

"Wait." She hurried over, brushing past him even as he moved into her room. "I don't need the carrier."

He couldn't take his eyes off the sketches. "You did all these?"

It was a significant amount of work. They weren't rough sketches. They'd been drawn in meticulous detail, large enough to really see the interlocking-chain design.

"It's nothing." She started gathering the papers, stacking them hurriedly, but carefully, too. Even as she juggled a cat in her arms.

"Nothing?" How could she write off such obvious hard work as nothing? "I hope you're not taking them to a competitor."

He was only half joking. Why else would she be trying to whisk them out of sight?

"Don't be silly." Skimming aside all the papers, she secured the cat in her bathroom, closing the door. "I saw the lunch spread out there." She yanked a black silk robe off the top of her suitcase, colorful clothes exploding out of it in every direction. "It looks delicious."

A curious response. Preston tucked it away, not wanting to risk upsetting the accord they were trying to find.

"I hoped there would be something you would like." He followed her back out into the living area.

She slipped her robe on, covering up her luscious bare legs. But when she turned and smiled at him, he had to admit that was just as much of a treat.

"As it happens, I am famished."

Later that evening, he twisted open a bottled water, waiting for Amie to finish dressing for their evening out—although thinking about her a door away showering? Not wise. Not when they had to spend so much time together.

He'd already changed into a tuxedo for the gala at the Natural History Museum. It was almost like taking Amie on a date—well, for him, anyway, since work permeated every aspect of his adult life.

A date?

Was that what this week was about? Starting up a relationship with her in spite of the fact he was fifteen years her senior—and her boss? Damn it, he didn't want to be that cliché. But he couldn't get her out of his mind.

The door to Amie's room clicked and…damn.

He set his bottle down slowly. The sight of her knocked the wind out of him. He'd spent so much time keeping professional distance, sometimes the impact of her just caught him unaware. She carried off a boho style all her own. One of a kind in so many ways.

She stood in the doorway, wearing a rhinestone halter top attached to a filmy peach skirt to the floor. Buff-colored cowboy boots peeked out with diamond anklets around them. Her hair, normally loose, was gathered in a tight braid and fell over her right shoulder. Only Amie could carry off such an eclectic pairing.

God, she was magnificent, and his body fired to life in answer. Who was he kidding? He noticed her every minute of every day—whether she was in no makeup and a T-shirt, or dressed to impress.

He pulled a rose from the arrangement on the wet bar. "You look damn hot and I bet you know it."

"Your flattery overwhelms me." She rolled her eyes but took the flower anyway, bringing it to her nose and inhaling. "Mmm."

"Plenty of people flatter you. You want to be respected for more than your looks or being a McNair, and I see that. Now, let's go wow the business world." He extended his elbow.

She stared at him in confusion for three blinks of her long eyelashes before she tucked her hand around his arm. "Lead the way."

He guided her to the penthouse elevator and tapped the button, the touch of her hand searing through his jacket. "I meant it when I said your work speaks for itself, no last name needed."

"Thank you, Preston. I appreciate that, truly," she said as the door slid open and they stepped inside. Together. "You know all about my family—thanks to our infamous nepotism—"

"I didn't say your family doesn't deserve their jobs—well, other than your father." He shrugged, wondering why he felt the need to shoot himself in the foot. "Sorry if that offends you."

"I can't condemn you for speaking the obvious." She snapped the bud off the long stem and tucked the flower into her long braid that draped over her shoulder, anchoring it with ribbon at the end. "I'm curious, though... Back to our questions game, what about your family?"

He went still for an instant, weighing his words. "No chance of nepotism in my family. There was no family business to join into. My father worked for a waste disposal company, injured his back and went on disability. My mother worked for a cleaning service. Mostly cleaning condos for a real estate company."

"It sounds like they had a difficult time financially." She leaned back against a mirrored wall, the lights glinting off her sequined top.

They had, and he'd been so determined to do differently by his family, sometimes he'd forgotten the positive parts of his childhood. "My dad may have been laid up, but he studied with me every day. He wanted to make sure I had more choices than he did. Than my mother did."

"Where are they now?"

The floors counted down as they descended toward ground level where their car waited, elevator music tuned to the Mozart station.

"I bought them a condominium in Florida, complete with maid service." He may have failed his ex and his daughter, but he'd done right by his parents.

"You support them? That's really lovely."

"I have more than enough money. Why wouldn't I?" His gaze dipped to the small of her back, visible in the mirrored wall behind her.

"Not everyone would. Do you get to see them often?"

"Not as often as I would like." He pulled his eyes

back up to her face, lingering for a second on the rose tucked in her hair. "I think you owe me about a dozen questions."

"All right, then ask," she answered with an ease that said he was making progress breaking through the awkwardness between them.

There was a chance for…hell, who was he kidding? He wanted a chance to have her again. In a bed. The attraction wasn't going away. It increased every day and was wrecking their work environment. Tonight was just a reminder of how damn hard it was to be professional with her. He wanted to free her from the layers of fabric, feel her body against his again.

"I'm going to save my questions for later, after work." He swept his arm toward the lobby, already looking forward to the ride back up the elevator.

Amie had been a part of Diamonds in the Rough since graduating from college with a double major in art and business. But until recently, she hadn't given a lot of thought to the expanded business that went into marketing the product. She'd assumed the pieces would come together for her at the right time, especially after her cousin had stepped down to pursue his own dreams.

God, that was brave of him to do.

She felt like a coward right now, afraid to tell Preston about the baby. This week was supposed to be about finding that courage, and the more time she spent with him, the more questions she had.

She stepped out of the limo in front of the Natural History Museum, the red carpet filled with LA elite and top players in Hollywood. Diamonds in the Rough collections would be displayed throughout. The evening passed in a blur of schmoozing, seeing her rustic gem designs and others artfully showcased throughout the Southwest exhibit—beside everything, from a stuffed longhorn steer, to a locomotive light, to portraits of the diverse people who'd shaped Western history.

She was a part of this, the McNair legacy, and she couldn't deny Preston was in command. He owned the room, quietly and confidently, alongside some of the most famous men and women in the country. Hooking them. No doubt there would be Diamonds in the Rough pieces adorning actors and actresses at music and movie awards shows.

By the end of the night, she felt light, excited about the business in a way she couldn't recall since she'd been a child making a necklace with her grandfather. She just wished she knew what Preston thought of her designs when he'd seen those sketches earlier in the day. Why hadn't he said anything?

But he had been thoughtful so far on this trip. The questions game had helped her learn things about him. The lunch he'd ordered—so obviously full of chick food that he'd selected items with her in mind—had been a sweet gesture, and so welcome, considering that her appetite really kicked in later in the day.

The business part of the event was winding down and the attendees were free to explore the museum for the remaining hour the company had rented the venue. Amie hooked arms with Preston, wondering if maybe, just maybe, they were going to find level ground after all.

She stared upward in wonder at the butterfly exhibit. Monarchs and a zillion other kinds she'd never thought to learn the names of glided, landed, soared again. Her imagination took flight along with them. "This museum was a genius idea for the display."

"It's about art. You design art every bit as beautiful, Amie."

She stopped, turning to face him. "I think that's the nicest thing you've ever said to me."

A half smile ticked a dimple in his craggy, handsome face. "Considering how little we've talked, that's not saying much."

"You know, you haven't been exactly accessible, yourself." She wanted to touch him, to stroke those strands of gray at his temples and see if they had a different texture.

"What do you mean?" All hard edges, he made such a contrast to those delicate yellow butterflies drifting behind him.

"You're a broody and moody workaholic." Even with butterflies as a backdrop.

"I'm the boss. I have to maintain a certain professional distance, and I'm certainly not going to set a bad example by taking long lunches and checking out early," he said with more of that broody moody authority. His mouth formed a tight line that she wanted to tease open.

"It's more than that." She tilted her head to the side, wondering if it was her imagination that his eyes lingered on her outfit now. And had all night, even amidst the A-list guests with plunging necklines. The thought sent satisfaction and desire through her. "You're not the warm fuzzy, approachable type."

"No. I've staked my reputation on being a leader not a team player. Besides, I'm also fifteen years your senior. You realize that, right?"

Did that bother him? She hadn't thought about it beyond thinking how well he carried it. The gray streaks at his temples, the hard, defined angles in his face. And those keen, calculating eyes. The man exuded pure sex appeal and would no matter what age. But she couldn't just dismiss what he'd said.

"The years between our birth dates would be an issue if I was a teenager. Ew. And illegal. But I'm far beyond that stage of life. So I don't see it as an excuse for distant behavior—" she took the plunge for her baby "—outside the office."

His eyes narrowed. "So you're saying outside the office is okay?" He took a step closer, still not touching but near enough that one deep breath would brush her chest against his. "Because I was under the distinct impression you didn't want to pursue the relationship because I'm the boss. And quite frankly, I agree that's problematic on a lot of levels if not handled carefully."

"Of course," she murmured, having thought through all of them. "You're right."

He studied her for a long moment, eyes so perceptive she wondered if he could pluck her secret thoughts right out of her head. Instead, his voice lowered to a level that hummed along her skin.

"But you're open to discussion," he pressed. "What are we going to do about working at the same company when there's still this connection?"

A butterfly landed on his shoulder and in that moment he was so very approachable. So much so, she couldn't think about anything but how scared she'd been since that stick turned pink.

"I guess that's what this week is supposed to be about."

She sure hoped he had answers, because she couldn't seem to figure out any.

Only one answer ever sprang to her mind when she got this close to Preston. And it had a lot to do with what he called a "connection." On her end, it felt more like a riot of emotions combined with raw lust and—quite honestly—a little bit of magic.

What else could explain her attraction to the off-limits cowboy CEO with a butterfly on one shoulder?

She chewed her bottom lip and before she could second-guess herself, she arched up onto her toes for what could be the last kiss she would ever have with Preston.

Four

Preston had Amie back in his arms again and the feel of her was better than any memory he'd held on to of that night in the coatroom. And his memories had been pretty damn awesome.

Her lips parted under the press of his, yielding in a way that could only happen when they were kissing and she wasn't snapping at him, just purring. Right now, with her mouth under his, there were no arguments. No doubts. Even in her yielding, she was sure of herself. Of the kiss. The silken stroke of her tongue along his told him as much while he skimmed a touch down her bare arms and up again, her halter top giving him delicious access to her shoulders. The slender warmth of her neck.

He breathed her in, deepening the kiss.

The press of her curves against his body sent his pulse into overdrive. The exotic scent of her musk- and-clove perfume tempted him, begged him to touch her. Everywhere. He enjoyed the silkiness of her hair as he stroked his hands over her braid. But he needed to touch more of her. Needed to feel her skin against his. She leaned into his fingertips as he ran them down her spine. Her nimble fingers played along his neck and over his shoulders. Every touch sent snaps of electricity through him until he backed her into a wall, his body shielding them from view if anyone walked in.

He hadn't tasted her enough that first time. Hell, he could kiss her for days and not get enough of her taste. She was such a flash of bright color in his world that he could see her like a damn kaleidoscope even behind his eyelids as they kissed.

More than that, she intrigued him. This woman who was won over by butterflies more than flowers or extravagant gifts. So different than his other relationships. She was unique. Special. And he should be old enough to know better, but still, she drew him in. Age and their work connection and his own shortcomings in relationships be damned. He wanted her, ached to have her.

And from the way she moved, Preston could tell Amie wanted it too. Her touch spurred him to take the chance. He kissed along her neck, nipping her shoulder. "Let's go back to the hotel. That is completely not the workplace and a helluva lot roomier than a coat closet."

Her head fell back and she blinked fast, long black eyelashes fluttering to focus. "What?"

"I want to take my time with you." His hands glided down her bare arms slowly, resting finally on her hips. A smile snaked across his lips. "I want to live out every fantasy I wish we'd had time for two months ago."

"Ohmigosh." The fog from her eyes cleared and hor-ror replaced passion. "What did we just do?"

"We kissed. Like two consenting adults who've been going damn crazy with frustration for the past two months trying to ignore the connection." He was losing ground fast and needed her to understand. "This is not about a repeat of the coatroom. This is about two adults attracted to each other. That's all."

She raised an eyebrow, face turning cold. Like marble. "Do you sleep with every person you're attracted to?"

He hadn't considered she might wonder about his motivations. It seemed odd that such a confident, sexy woman could have insecurities, too, but as he thought back to those sketches she'd tried to hide from him, he had to wonder. "I meant it when I said I'm not a one-night-stand person and I believed you were being hon-est, too."

"You're saying we should…what?" She angled her head to the side, butterflies swirling behind her in a display. Her blue eyes steeled against him. "That we go on dates? That we sleep together?"

"Honestly? I was thinking we would do both." There would be issues to deal with, datingwise, but he wasn't a man who tolerated sneaking around.

"What about all the things you said earlier?" She backed out of his embrace and crossed her arms over her chest defensively. "You're my boss and older than I am. That you're not a team player."

Good question. And that meant she was considering it. He was closer to winning. "We keep our relationship separate when we're at work with a little less ice and obvious static. We're both professionals."

She shook her head, the rose slipping loose from

her braid. It tumbled to the floor behind her, landing silently. "It isn't that simple."

It felt simple enough to him, especially seeing the way her fingers trembled lightly as she skimmed them across her lips where he'd just kissed her. His gaze followed the path of that sensual touch, hungry to show her how very, very simple—elemental—this could be.

"Why not?" he asked instead, thirsty for more of her. "What's the harm in trying a date? Or more. See what happens? Can't be more awkward than the past two months."

Indecision flickered through her eyes, just a flash before she held up a hand. "Don't try to win me over with your corporate pitch. I am not okay with the way you've cleared house and tampered with the family culture at McNair. You can save your closing-deal number. I know how you operate, and who knows, maybe my head's next on the chopping block."

"That's not in the cards," he said without hesitation.

Her throat moved in a slow swallow of relief. "Well, I'm not some account to win over."

"You most definitely are not." She was more. So much more.

Amie shook her head. "Save it."

A tight line smoothed her plump lips into an expression that he couldn't readily identify. Pain? Hesitation? He wasn't sure. And while he realized he would have to put his plans on hold for now, he was not giving up. Not on this woman.

Amie broke his gaze, turned around and made for the door. She stepped on the flower, smearing the red petals on the ground.

Preston stared at the ground, breathing in the scent of roses for a moment while he contemplated his next move.

The ride back to the hotel in the limousine was awkward, to say the least. Amie couldn't stop thinking about the kiss in the butterfly gallery. How much she wanted to take Preston up on his proposition. In fact, she very well might have if she hadn't been pregnant. But she was and she had to keep that in mind at all times for her baby's sake.

Preston sat across from her, giving her space. Although she could sense he was only biding his time. She'd watched him at work often enough to know his tactics. Telling him to back down wouldn't work. She needed to come up with a plan of her own.

Soon.

Her cell phone rang inside her pewter handbag. The bag, while stylish, was full of essentials. She batted around a mess of receipts and makeup, digging for the ringing phone. In the seat next to her, she dumped her lip gloss, mints and amethyst-and-pearl compact. Finally, the purse was empty enough to find her phone. She fumbled with the turquoise clasp. Her grandmother's name flashed across the screen. Her gut clenched in fear.

She grabbed the phone and answered fast. "Gran, it's late in Texas. What's the matter?"

Preston's forehead creased and he looked at her, a question in his eyes. She averted her gaze. Now wasn't the time to worry about Preston. Not when her grandmother was this sick.

"Nothing's wrong, dear." Her grandmother's voice

came across weaker but steady. "I'm just calling to see how the party at the museum went."

"The party? You're calling for an after-action report now?" she asked incredulously. "It's after midnight there, Gran. We can talk tomorrow. You should be asleep."

Her grandmother snorted on the other end of the line. "All I do is lie around in bed and rest. It wrecks my sense of day and night."

"Are you feeling all right?" Amie lowered her voice, wishing for a moment of privacy. Her grandmother's illness was hard for her to deal with. She hated to think of her grandmother awake in pain.

"You just saw me this weekend. I'm the same."

Dying. Moments ticking away while Amie was stuck going to parties. It wasn't fair. She wanted to be at her side. To soak up the precious, borrowed time with her grandmother.

"And I'm going to worry about you every single hour of every day because I love you and you're so very important to me."

"You're a sweet girl. My only granddaughter. I was so excited when you were born."

"Sweet? Me?" She laughed softly. "Not really, but then neither are you. I like to think I inherited my feistiness from you."

Her grandmother chuckled along with her, then laughed harder until she coughed. Clearing her throat, she continued, "I am proud of you and I believe you can make this work. Now, tell me. How is it going?"

"The LA party was a success. The museum setting was brilliant." The kiss with Preston was incredible, but that part would not appear in any reports. "The photographer took lots of photos. You should have them on your computer to look through in the morning. If you're still having trouble resting, some pictures may have already arrived."

"Photos of you with Preston? I want to see how the two of you work together."

Alarms sounded in her head. Had her grandmother picked up on some vibe between her and Preston? She couldn't possibly know about the baby. Amie settled on a simple answer. "We were a unified front for the company."

"So you're working through the differences that fast? I'm not buying it, dear."

"We're trying." She looked across the limo, her eyes meeting his. Had he been watching her so intently the whole time? Concern etched in his face. Genuine concern. It'd be so easy to let her guard fall, even now. "For you, Gran. Now, please, get some rest. We won't let you down."

The line disconnected and Amie realized more than her baby's well-being was at stake here. Her grandmother's peace of mind needed to stay in the forefront. They needed to smooth things over. And fast. She could make it through the week, smile for pictures with him. Amie couldn't afford to weaken again around Preston. She had to stay strong and make sure every step was taken on her terms. She needed to reclaim some control.

Preston angled back, his arms along the leather limo seat. "Everything okay?"

"Sure. No crisis." The last thing she wanted to tell him was that she suspected her grandmother could have ulterior motives beyond solidifying business relations. "She just wanted to check in."

"And that's all?" His hazel eyes narrowed in disbelief. The shadows in the limousine softened his features, making him seem more approachable. "I don't think so."

"What are you? Psychic?" She gripped the edges of the seat as the limo turned a corner. The driver took the corner hard, and she lurched toward Preston.

"I just know." He lifted his index finger to the side of his temple and tapped twice. "It's part of what makes me the boss," he said, his confidence filling the seat as tangibly as his broad shoulders.

"That—" she paused for effect, then grinned "—and your arrogance."

He laughed, apparently not daunted in the least. "Confidence is important. You're one to talk, by the way."

She opted to ignore that part. "Aren't you going to ask why she called so late?"

The smile faded from his handsome face. "Tell me."

"She's having trouble sleeping because she's in bed so much." And Amie wanted to be there with her to keep her company, but her grandmother wanted her here for whatever reason. For a test. "It tears me up inside to think of her confined like that. She's always been such a vibrant, dynamic woman. She's the one who taught me to ride. Alex, Stone and I would spend hours out on the trails with her and Gramps."

"I'm sorry. This is such an unfair way for her life to end."

"I'm grateful she can still talk, that she's still herself. The thought of…"

The limousine stopped short, and Amie fell forward, landing her onto Preston's lap. He reached out to catch her instinctively. Heat flooded her cheeks as his warm hands helped her back to an upright position. This was exactly the kind of situation she needed to guard herself against. Thank heaven they had arrived at the hotel. Amie was exhausted with worry for her grandmother, her child and her feelings.

She peered out the window only to realize they'd stopped a couple of blocks short of the hotel. Preston frowned, but she was closer to the window separating them from the chauffeur. She tapped on the pane, signaling the driver.

The window slid opened. "Yes, Mr. Armstrong? Miss McNair?"

"Is there a problem?"

The uniformed driver scratched under his hat. "There's a pileup that has traffic blocked ahead of us and there's no backing up. I'm afraid we're stuck until it clears. The minifridge is stocked."

Alone? In the limo with Preston for who knew how long?

Amie snatched up her pewter clutch bag. "We'll just walk. The hotel is only two blocks and this highway congestion is never going to let up."

The chauffeur looked to Preston, who shrugged. "Whatever the lady wants."

Amie stepped out into the warm night. Whatever she wanted? If only life could be that simple.

Preston shot out of the limo, stunned at how fast she'd bolted. No way in hell was he letting her walk around the streets of LA alone, regardless of how safe the area was supposed to be. It was still a city, far different from the open spaces of Texas. Besides that, she looked exactly like what she was—an extraordinarily beautiful and wealthy woman, both of which could attract the wrong sort of attention. Five sprints later, he'd caught her, her sequined top glinting in the night.

He shortened his strides to measure his pace to Amie's as he scanned the traffic-jammed street. The famous LA traffic was no joke. People honked their horns, and music with heavy bass from a parked car filled the night air. The hotel was located in a good section of LA, but his instincts still stayed on alert. There were plenty of places, even in the good areas of the city that could be a threat to two pedestrians. He placed a palm on the small of her back possessively as they walked. He glanced at her, narrowing his eyes and daring her to argue. "If you don't want my hand on you then we get back in the limo."

She sighed, tucking her handbag against her side. "We need to set some ground rules for the rest of this trip."

At least she was still talking to him. That was progress over the past two months of the great chill. "Such as?"

He continued to scan the area as they walked down the empty sidewalk. They had made it one block away from the limo. The street signs were caked brown from the smog. To a native Oklahoma kid, cities like LA felt dirty and overcrowded, even in the upscale areas. The sooner they were back at the hotel, the better. Maybe he could convince her to stay for a glass or two of wine in the hotel's restaurant.

"We have to work together for years to come," she said with her chin jutting, exposing her elegant neck.

He wanted to kiss her, starting at her neck. The taste of her two months ago and in the exhibit this evening wasn't nearly enough. Preston's attention wandered from her neck to the seductive swish of her filmy skirt.

Her boot heels clicked against the pavement, a steady drumming sound that matched the evenness of her voice. "We need to figure out how to make that happen without the attraction interfering."

"I still don't see what that has to do with denying the pull between us altogether."

"You mean have an affair."

"We *are* adults. Sex happens sometimes." The more he thought about it, the more it made sense. Even though they worked together, there was an equality to their stance since her family was the major stockholder. And she clearly didn't want a long-term relationship, thank God, since he'd already been there, wrecked that with his ex-wife. "Fighting the attraction isn't working. An affair makes sense."

"That brings me back to my original point. Affairs more often than not end…messy." She clutched her purse to her stomach. "We can't afford that."

"Then we agree that when the time comes to move on, we'll be cordial." He guided her past other pedestrians making their way down the sidewalk. Blue-and-red lights flashed in the distance as first responders pushed through the backed-up traffic to get to the three-car pileup.

"Preston, I hear what you're saying, but it's not that simple anymore." Her throat moved with a long swallow. "We can't afford to take that risk. The stakes are too high. Far too high."

There was such worry in her eyes, an unmistakable fear. Panic tore at her face.

He squeezed her elbow lightly. "I think that until

we face this head-on and give it a try, the tension will only get worse and interfere with the job all the more."

"Spoken like a man who doesn't take no for an answer."

"I didn't imagine what just happened or what happened two months ago."

She glanced up at him, her eyes full of more of that worry he didn't understand—but a yearning he understood all too well.

Chewing her bottom lip, she glanced at him. "Preston, can we go back to the original plan of getting to know each other better and take it from there?"

"Are you asking me to win you over?" The prospect filled him with a rush of excitement and hope.

"No," she said quickly, "I didn't mean that, exactly. Just…just… I'm asking you to be honest."

He measured his words, searching for the best way to win his way around her. "Okay, but on one condition."

"What would that be?" she asked warily.

"That we use this time together as dates. Real, honest-to-God, get-to-know-each-other dates. You'll see firsthand that we can balance work and romance."

Her jaw dropped. "Dating? You're serious."

"Absolutely, take our time."

She fidgeted with her purse gripped in her hands. "And when you say take our time, how long are you talking?"

"However long it takes. Trust me, I don't take this lightly. I'm not the type to let relationships into the workplace, never have been. You're just that damn amazing."

"Flattery already? I haven't agreed yet, so you can hold back on the wooing." For the first time since the kiss in the exhibit, Amie looked relaxed. Receptive.

The smile on her face reached her eyes, setting them aglow in the muted streetlight. She shoved him with her shoulder playfully. This was the Amie he wanted to get to know.

"I only speak the truth." God, she was mesmerizing. So much so, it was hard as hell to see anything but the stars shining in her deep blue eyes.

So hard he almost missed the shadowy figure lunging from behind a billboard. The man was broad, built and hardened by the streets. His frenetic eyes focused on Amie with a repugnant leer. On instinct, Preston stepped in front of her. Crooks like this never risked leaving people alive to identify them, especially when drugs were making their decisions for them.

The man loomed in front of them, a knife in hand, waving it menacingly. Erratically. "Give me your cash and jewelry now and nobody gets hurt."

Five

"Amie, get back." Preston pushed her behind him, the street lamp casting a halogen halo over the man with a knife, his face shadowed by the brim of a ball cap. "We don't want anyone to get hurt."

Fear chilled Amie so thoroughly her boots felt frozen to the pavement. She stared at the jagged-edge blade glistening in the night.

"Then pass over your money, dude, and quit screwing around here." The broad shouldered young guy stood close, looking from side to side, jittery. The rest of the world oblivious or uncaring. Or perhaps too busy rubbernecking over the three-car pileup to notice a simple purse snatcher by a trash can.

In a flash, Preston swept a foot behind the guy, knocking him to the ground, stunning Amie with the speed and power. Preston stomped a foot on the crook's wrist, pressing until the criminal screamed. His fist unfurled and he released the jagged knife.

The clatter of metal on concrete released Amie from her daze. She sprinted toward the flashing lights at the car accident. Surely there had to be a cop there who could assist.

"Help, please," she called out, waving one hand and hitching the hem of her layered skirt with the other. "Someone tried to rob us. My…boss has him restrained. The man had a knife. My…date…has him restrained."

A few heads turned, two rescue workers returning to their efforts to dislodge a woman from a smashed-up car. But one cop disengaged from the accident scene.

"Yes, ma'am?" The policeman with a shaved head and steely jaw jogged closer.

Thank God. She waved for him to follow her.

"Over here, by the closed toy store." Her heart in her throat, she raced back to Preston.

A small crowd had gathered around the fallen thief, suddenly interested, after all. The onlookers hungrily digested the scene, pointing and murmuring at Preston, who had the young man pinned to the ground with his knee planted on the guy's back, gripping the assailant's hands.

The officer and Amie pushed past the crowd, walking with determined footsteps to Preston. Relief deflated her fear, but even relief didn't keep her knees from trembling as she thought of how wrong this could have gone. And she had a baby to think about now. Preston's baby. If something had happened to either of them… She started toward him, needing to touch him and feel him vibrantly alive. But he shook his head, keeping her at bay until he passed over the crook.

"Officer," Preston said, "that's his knife there. You'll find his prints since he didn't bother to wear gloves. I didn't touch it."

The policeman knelt beside them and secured the man's hands with cuffs. "I've got this now, sir. I'll be right back to take your statements." He read the guy his rights and walked him to a police cruiser.

Standing, Preston straightened his jacket and cupped her shoulder to steer her away from the subdued criminal. "Are you hurt, Amie?"

"I should be asking you that." She pressed her hands to her chest, vaguely aware of camera flashes in the background. Photos of the wreck? Cell phones were everywhere these days. "You're the one who took on the man with the knife. Thanks to you, there's not a scratch on me. You acted so quickly. I thought we would have just handed over our money."

"He was high on something." Preston's jaw flexed with tension. "I couldn't trust him to walk away, not even in this crowd."

"I'm just glad you were here with me. I'm sorry I forced us to walk and put you in danger."

"It could have happened anywhere, anytime. All that matters is you're okay." He clasped her elbow and nodded to the policeman. "We should go inside to wait for the cops to take our statement. The last thing I want is for someone else to try a repeat."

"Of course. I know I've already apologized, but I am so sorry for leaving the limo." Guilt pinched tighter than her boots as she strode through the lobby doors of their hotel, passed a small group of guests peering out the windows onto the street outside. The posh interior felt like a different world. "Where did you learn to defend yourself like that?"

"I grew up in a neighborhood where you had to look out for yourself." He gestured to a green velvet sofa by the window overlooking the street.

"Still, that was such a risky move to make." She sank onto the couch and smoothed her skirt. "You could have been injured—or worse."

"Less risky than trusting a twitchy user to let us go unharmed. My only concern was keeping you safe." He sketched a finger down the braid trailing over her shoulder. "I could see in his eyes he was never going to let us walk away and risk having us ID him. He wanted you. I couldn't let that happen."

Unable to resist, she leaned her cheek against his hand. "Thank you for keeping us safe."

"Us?"

She bit her lip, realizing she'd almost let it slip about the baby at a totally awkward and public time. "Us— as in you and me." She stood quickly when the door to the hotel opened, relieved at the intrusion. "I think I see the officer coming this way to speak with us now."

Amie sat on her bed, cloaked in her favorite black silk robe, absently stroking her cat. The cat purred loudly, but refused to lie down on her lap. He was fidgety.

She felt just like Roscoe. He refused to sit down, to commit to a direction. Just like her. She couldn't stop thinking about this evening, either. About the whole varied experience. Her kiss with Preston. Her grandmother's desires. Her child. The man with the knife. All of it swirled around her head.

"Oh, Roscoe, what am I supposed to do?"

The cat nudged her hand in response. "Thanks, kitty. That's clearly very helpful. Great advice."

She stopped petting the cat, pushed herself off the bed and made her way to the minifridge. Water. She needed some water.

Things with Preston were more complicated than ever. She wanted to be with him. Wanted to let herself give in to him.

It wasn't that easy. Her own happiness wasn't the only consideration. She unscrewed the water bottle cap and took a swig of water.

Roscoe slinked off the bed and rubbed up against Amie's legs, threading around her feet with determination. He let out a low mew. He sounded more like a kitten than an old cat.

"All right, Roscoe, let's get you settled for the night. I've got your favorite treats."

Whenever they traveled, Amie made sure to pack the best assortment of toys for the cat. He was so loyal, her constant companion. She dug around Roscoe's traveling bag and pulled out a can of tuna, a bowl, a can opener and a blue mouse toy.

Absently, Amie drained the tuna water into the bowl and set it on the ground. The cat rushed the bowl, eager to lap up the treat. Roscoe didn't actually like the fish, just the water. Small indulgences.

Which, if she were being honest, is what she wanted with Preston. A small bit of fun.

It was more than that though. The way he looked at her tonight when her grandmother had called. He had such genuine concern in that handsome face of his. In those kind hazel eyes. And he had saved her. Stood up to that mugger without a moment's hesitation. So protective of her already.

And that was part of the problem. If she had let it slip that she was pregnant, Preston would stay close to her for the baby's sake. She would never be able to tell what he really felt for her. And selfish as it was, she wanted to know. Needed to know.

Glancing at the clock, Amie realized she was late in giving Roscoe his insulin injections. She readied the needle, scooped Roscoe up and pinched the extra skin around his neck. The cat was perfectly still.

"Good boy. You're such a good boy. I always know what to expect from you, Roscoe," she said softly as she slid the needle into his scruff.

"Brave kitty. That wasn't so bad, was it?" She capped the needle and rubbed under his chin. Roscoe circled once on her lap, sat down and purred.

She still had to figure out Preston. Tomorrow, in New York City, she would get to know him better. Which was what she had started to consider just before she'd realized she was pregnant. Baby announcements could wait a while longer. There was something about him that made her want to hold out. Just a little longer.

Preston hadn't found much sleep after the holdup. Instead, he had paced restlessly around the suite replaying events and how damn wrong the evening could have gone. How something could have happened to Amie. And how deeply that would have affected him.

She'd come to mean more to him than he'd realized. So much more.

He was still processing that after their flight across the country to New York City the next morning. Their event wasn't until tomorrow evening, which normally meant he would fill the free day with work. However, he found himself wanting to spend every moment with Amie. When he couldn't sleep the night before, he'd heard her moving about in her room for a long while, but just as he weakened and started to knock, all noise ceased. She settled for the night, leaving him to his thoughts and an aching need to be with her. The trauma of the attack must have worn her out, because she slept during most of the flight, too.

Now that he had New York City at his disposal, he didn't intend to waste an instant of his time alone here with her.

Figuring out what to do for one of the wealthiest women in the country hadn't been easy, but then he'd always enjoyed a challenge.

He'd arranged for a rickshaw to take them to Central Park to attend a Wild West film festival. The muggy day had eased with the setting sun, a pleasant breeze added to the wind from the ride. The *click, click, click* of the cyclist pedaling along the street was rhythmic, lulling. Amie sat beside him in killer shorts and heels with a flowy shirt that the wind molded to all her beautiful curves.

She leaned back, her high ponytail sleek and swinging with the pace of the horses. Her eyes took in the scenery. "I love New York, I always have."

"Always?" He propped a foot up on the other seat across from them, not remembering the last time he'd relaxed in the city. Hell, most people he knew probably wouldn't even recognize him in khaki shorts and a polo shirt. He'd spent all his time in planes, boardrooms and carefully chosen social functions for years.

"My grandparents used to bring Alex and me here as kids. We would see a show, do some shopping." Her blue eyes turned sentimental as they passed Rockefeller Center, a lighter blue as she offered him a small smile.

"I can see why that would give the town good memories."

She glanced at crowded streets as tourists jostled for pictures. "My grandmother always let me choose my own clothes, no worries about impressing a pageant judge."

"You didn't enjoy any part of the pageants?"

"To be honest, I did at first. I liked that my mom spent time with me. I enjoyed the attention. And I really enjoyed getting to have a Mountain Dew and Pixy Stix if the pageant ran past bedtime and I needed a pick-me-up." She shrugged sheepishly, her shoulder brushing his in the confines of the small rickshaw. "Later, though, I wanted to enter the competitions that included talent and grades and community service. But my mother told me that would be a waste of time. I stood a better chance at the ones based only on looks." She stopped short and held up an elegant hand, a silver bracelet wrapped from wrist to elbow. "I don't mean that to sound vain. Scratch everything I said. I shouldn't have—"

"I heard what you meant." And he couldn't imagine ever having said something like that to his daughter. That kind of behavior was inexcusable. "You're clearly a talented artist and intelligent individual."

She snorted inelegantly. "You have to say that because my grandmother owns the company."

"No, actually, I don't," he said with a raised eyebrow as they turned in to Central Park, the sound of street musicians drifting on the wind as the sunset hour turned the sky to golds and pinks. "If I didn't believe in your work I would have moved you to another department."

"Even if that made my grandmother angry?" she pressed.

Did she really think he was only pursuing her for her grandmother's approval? He could clear that much up at least. "My condition to signing on was I have complete authority over hiring."

"But my father still works for the company and we know he doesn't do anything." Her cheeks flushed with color.

And he understood that. She had one helluva work ethic he respected.

"Your father doesn't get a salary from the company coffers so it's not an issue for me. He has an office where he holds social meetings with possible connections. I can live with that."

"It's awkward," she said through clenched teeth, absently toying with her bracelet. "I don't want to be an embarrassment."

He slid his arm along the back of the leather seat and cupped her shoulders. "There's not a chance anyone can miss your work ethic and talent. The other designers are solid, and the occasional design from your cousin adds variety. But the sales numbers for your designs speak for themselves, putting you at the top of the heap."

She glanced at him, her mouth quivering, tempting him. "Thank you. I appreciate that."

"Just stating business." Which meant that wouldn't be a good time to kiss her. He searched for a distracting subject to keep him from kissing her in front of all of New York. Not that anyone would care. "What about vacations with your parents?"

"We went to my pageants and my brother's rodeos together."

"But what about vacations?"

"They took those on their own to have together time as a couple, which is great, of course. And if Alex or I won, then all the better."

So her parents only had time for her and her brother if they were competing like show horses? He didn't like the sound of that at all. No wonder she was so concerned with rising to the top of the company. It wasn't about success but the only way she would know to feel valued.

She rested a hand lightly on his knee. "What about you? What kind of vacations did you go on as a kid?"

His body leaped in response to her touch and it took him a second to focus on her question. "My folks didn't have much money, but we went camping and trail riding. You may remember me telling you my mom worked for a cleaning service. She worked overtime cleaning offices for a stable, so we got discount rates and we could ride. It was actually therapeutic for my dad's injury."

"Your mom sounds awesome." She smiled with that million-watt grin that had stolen his breath from across a room. "So you're the real-deal cowboy. Is that what brought you to Diamonds in the Rough?"

"It was part of the allure of the job offer." He liked riding to unwind after a long day at the office. It gave him peace of mind.

"So, where are we going?"

"Wild West film festival in Central Park. Our first date."

"Date?" Her delicately arched eyebrows shot upward.

"What we talked about last night. Dating. Spending

time together. How did you put it?" He scratched his temple, then pointed. "I'm 'wooing' you."

The bicyclist braked to a stop close to the Sheep Meadow portion of the park, an open field teeming with people, with plenty of visible security. After last night's scare with the purse snatcher, he'd wondered if he should just lock them both up in their suite. But he also knew too well he couldn't control everything. So he would keep her close. Which was how he wanted her.

Snagging a folded blanket and tucking it under his arm, he jumped to the ground and extended a hand for her. She stepped down gracefully, her slim fingers resting in his, her unique silver-and-turquoise ring a walking advertisement for her talents. They walked side by side through the crowd to find a seat. Some were in chairs but others sprawled on blankets. His preference for tonight. He saw her eyes landing on a food vendor and he waved for an order of pizza and bottled waters before they sat down for tonight's first feature under the stars.

He spread the red plaid blanket while she arranged the food. Families and couples dotted the field. A few strollers and kids running in the last light of day. Some people had brought extravagant picnics, complete with linen, silver and candelabra. But most of the attendees had just showed up in jeans with a blanket. Amie seemed content with their spot. She extended her legs and bit off the end of a slice of pepperoni pizza, chasing the oozing cheese with her mouth. Groaning. Pleasure obvious.

"Oh my God, this is the best piece of pizza I have ever eaten in my life."

"So you're a sucker for a pizza pie," he said, lifting up a piece for himself. "I did not expect that."

"And I didn't expect this for a date, but it's perfect. Just what I needed after all the stuffiness of the airplane travel and galas."

"I thought you would enjoy the fresh-air venue after so much time indoors."

She nodded, swiping her lips with a napkin. "The downside to office work is missing being outside. My brother managed to blend both, running the ranch."

"I agree one hundred percent. That's part of what drew me to Texas and this job." In fact, he'd had it written into the contract that he would have access to the ranch. "Someday I want to build a big spread of my own to live the kind of life I dreamed of as a kid. My folks could come visit. At any rate, tonight I figured the outdoor ride would work better, too, in the event of another traffic jam."

"Better than being stuck in the limo." She tipped back a swig of water.

"Spoken like a person who's grown up wealthy." He couldn't resist commenting, even though that had been his life for a long time, too.

He'd never forgotten his roots. Or how lucky he was today.

She crinkled her nose and set aside her water. "I guess that came out snobby."

"Not snobby. Just…a sign that you grew up privileged."

She tipped her head. "Is that a problem for you?"

"It's just a challenge figuring out ways to romance you." He threaded his fingers through her ponytail.

"And we've established you like a challenge." Her eyes held his.

"Don't start with the negative." He tapped her lips. "Just be in the moment."

"You really are charming under all that gruff business exterior." Her mouth moved against his fingertips. "How did you stay single so long?"

His hand fell away and he looked forward at the blank movie screen, due to glow to life at any minute. "I was married, but we got divorced ten years ago."

She went still beside him, her long legs straight beside his, almost touching. "I'm sorry."

"Me, too." And he was. He hated how much they'd hurt and disappointed each other. Most of all, he hated what had happened to their child. His throat threatened to close. "But we married too young. We gave it a good shot, and it just didn't work out."

"Do you have children?"

His blood turned to ice in his veins. "I have no children."

He could practically hear her thinking through that. His heart slammed harder.

"Do you not like kids?" she asked, her voice tentative.

"I like kids fine." He paused, stared up at the sky then back at her, needing to be honest if this stood a chance of…what? Anything. So he told her as much as he could force past his lips. "I had a daughter. She died."

"Oh, Preston, that's so sad." She rested her hand on top of his on the blanket. "Do you mind if I ask what happened?"

His publicity people had done a damn good job keeping those details hidden from the public, even better than he'd known if the McNairs hadn't discovered those details in the background search they'd undoubtedly conducted before hiring him.

"It was an accident." He cleared his throat. He couldn't talk about this, not the rest. He scrambled for something, anything— "Look, the first movie is starting."

A black-and-white film crackled to life on the screen, the projected version maintaining the authenticity of the original as the Western-style font blazed across the screen with a lasso frame decorating the title. It wouldn't be the first time Preston had lost himself in a place where Gary Cooper and Roy Rogers could still make sense of the world.

She looked as if she might press for more, so he slid his arm along her back and pulled her to his side, wanting just to be with her. Enjoy this.

"Amie. Movie. Okay?"

She relented, leaning against his chest with a sigh. "Right. Sure. I didn't mean to push you to talk about something painful."

"It's all right. Another time, maybe."

For now, he had her in his arms and that helped ease the pain inside him in a way he hadn't felt in a long time. A way he looked forward to exploring more fully when they returned to their hotel.

Six

Nerves pattered in Amie's stomach as the elevator doors slid closed on their way up to their penthouse suite in Midtown Manhattan. The evening in the park had been amazing, romantic, fun. Everything a first real date should be. And surprisingly, he hadn't made a move on her other than sliding his arm around her, being a gentleman but undeniably interested in her. She hadn't felt so mellow and happy in…she couldn't remember when.

Was this the real Preston? Was this what they could have had if she'd dated him rather than impulsively leaping into a coat closet with him? God, that night was so surreal now. But they'd actually been together, no denying their impulsive coupling.

She leaned back against the mirrored wall, just looking at him, soaking in the sight of him. Casual. Approachable. His hazel eyes softened as he held her gaze. Heat flushed through her. Everything felt right. Natural. Could she just indulge for a little while longer and see where it went?

The high-speed elevator brought them to their floor in record time, the doors opening on the west half of the tower, thanks to the private code they'd keyed in for their room. The east-side doors went to a different suite.

She took a deep breath and reached to take Preston's arm as she stepped off the elevator on their private quarters. Only to have Roscoe bolt into the elevator—something that shouldn't have happened because she'd secured the kitty in her bathroom before she'd left.

Alarms sounded in her head as she squeezed Preston's hand. She went rigid, cold. "Someone's been in our suite. I locked up Roscoe…maybe a maid let him out?"

Preston's arm shot out to block her path. "After what happened in LA, I'm not taking any chances. Get back in the elevator. Call Security while I go in. What the hell is it with all the security around these places?"

He charged forward and her stomach knotted with fear for him. The events of last night replayed in her head. She had the baby to consider, but she couldn't just leave him here. She held the elevator door open while reaching for her cell phone.

Across the room, someone sat up on the sofa. A familiar someone in jeans, cowboy boots and a plain black T-shirt.

Her twin.

"Hey there, sister." Alex stood, sweeping a hand through his dark brown hair. "I happened to be in the neighborhood and figured I would say hello."

* * *

Suspicion seared through Preston as he strode toward Amie's twin brother. Here. In Manhattan. In their suite. Did the guy have some kind of brotherly radar that Preston was making progress with Amie? Their night at the park had been everything he'd hoped it could be.

He'd had plans to take things further tonight, but clearly that had been blocked by a towering, suspicious cowboy sibling.

Preston sauntered toward Alex McNair, aware of Amie rushing up behind him. "What are you doing here in New York?"

Alex extended an arm and hooked his sister in for a quick hug before backing up and keeping his arm draped protectively over her shoulders. "I brought Nina and Cody to see a matinee on Broadway, like Gran and Gramps used to do with us. Cody okayed the plan once he heard the show has animals in it. And my fiancée could use some pampering with a shopping trip in New York, some spa time along with that show. Amie, you're welcome to join in."

Amie narrowed her eyes, sticking her brother with an accusatory stare. "And you just happened to choose the day I would be here as well? The hotel staff must have fond memories of you from past trips that they gave you access to my suite."

Her brother shrugged. "I think our family has made a favorable—and lucrative—impression on the management in the past. I spent almost a whole summer here once when I was determined to leave the rodeo life behind." He huffed out a long breath. "Anyhow, there's the Diamonds in the Rough show tomorrow. I figured why not bring Nina and show our support for the family business."

"Where is Nina?"

"Settling into the other penthouse suite next door, getting Cody unpacked and oriented before he goes to sleep." Nina's son had autism and changes in routine could be difficult.

"I'll see if she needs help." She slipped from under his arm, but pinned him with a laser gaze of matching blue eyes. "But we're still going to talk later."

As Alex gave her the code to access the other suite, Preston couldn't help but watch the sway of her hips when she left, wishing like hell this evening could have ended differently.

Alex cleared his throat. "That's my sister you're ogling. Eyes up."

Preston pivoted on his heels and walked to the bar, pulling out two beers. The last thing he needed was this oversize cowboy brother breathing down his neck personally—or professionally. "Did your grandmother send you to check on the event tomorrow?"

And did this have something to do with the McNair matriarch calling her granddaughter yesterday? Preston passed his uninvited guest a longneck.

Alex took the Belgian brew. "My grandmother has nothing to do with this. It's all me. I'm checking in on my sister. You and her together?" He shook his head. "That worries me."

"Amie is an adult. Perhaps you should listen to what she has to say on the subject." He tipped back the yeasty brew.

"I realize that. Doesn't make me any less of a protective brother." He took a long drag from the bottle.

"You're known for being a distant dude. I don't want my sister to get hurt. She puts on a tough act, but she's been pushed around by the family for too long."

"I think you underestimate your sister if you think anyone can push her around." Preston tilted his head to the side.

Alex's eyebrows shot up in surprise. "You have a point there. But that's the Amie you know now and you haven't known her that long." The child's voice echoed from the other suite and Alex looked away quickly. "Let's go next door to check on them. I want to make sure Cody's still okay with all the change." Preston wanted to push for more now, but Alex had already started for the door leading to the second penthouse through the shared elevator. He punched in the code. The doors swept open to reveal the two women sitting on the living room floor with a young, blond-haired boy—Cody. An intricate puzzle lay on the coffee table.

The suite was much the same as its mate, other than the use of silver and blues rather than reds and golds for the lavish accommodations. Preston hadn't grown up in this sort of world, but he'd earned his way into the life of the rich and famous. He hoped he'd kept his feet and priorities planted, much like the young mom over there with her child. There hadn't been much time for him to get to know Alex's recent fiancée and her son, but he'd been impressed by her down-to-earth ways and her devotion to her child.

Amie glanced up, her eyes lighting as she looked at Preston before she shifted her attention back to the puzzle self-consciously. Nina reached up to clasp hands with Alex briefly, connecting without taking her attention off her four-year-old son. Alex kissed the top of her head full of red curls before dropping to sit on the window seat overlooking the buildings lighting up the night skyline.

Preston joined him, curious what this gathering held in store—and what he could learn about Amie.

She helped Cody match pieces in the puzzle, a Monet image far more advanced than a four-year-old could normally put together. But Mariah had told him Cody was a savant at art, and Amie had a gift for helping tap into that connection with the child. She was good with kids and that touched something in him he hadn't thought about in a long while.

Alex set down his bottle on the window ledge. "You asked about my sister," he said softly. "Do you want to know as a boss or for more personal reasons?"

Might as well be honest. He wasn't having any luck hiding his attraction to her. And maybe Alex would respect the straight talk. "This has nothing to do with business. I would like to get to know her better."

"Okay then." Alex nodded slowly, his eyes settling on his sister, fiancée and future stepson. "Did Amie ever tell you about the time Stone and I put Kool-Aid in Amie's showerhead right before the Miss Stampede Queen pageant? I didn't think she would ever forgive either of us for turning her hair pink. Not to mention her skin."

Where was he going with this story? "Seriously?"

"Mom never could figure out which one of us to blame. I did it, but she was convinced Stone egged me on." A smile twitched.

"And the truth?"

His grin faded. "I wanted to help her, and Stone was more of a rebel, the idea man behind the prank. He left a gag book open to a particular page right on my desk."

Preston envisioned Amie stepping out of that shower covered in pink dye—um, better not to think overmuch on that image. "I bet Amie was furious."

"Not really. She wasn't as into the pageant gig as Mom likes to think. It was pretty much the only way she could get attention from our mother."

"That sucks."

"It was worse when she was little. As she got older, she started to rebel." He rolled the beer bottle between his palms. "When we were seventeen, she didn't want to win the Miss Honey Bee Pageant—and given how many pageants she'd won in the past, it wasn't arrogant of her to assume she would run away with that crown. But back to that time. She didn't want to go because the Honey Bee Queen had to attend the county fair and she wouldn't be able to attend homecoming."

"What did you do that time?" He was getting an image of these three growing up together, protecting each other from dysfunctional parents but bonded by the love of their grandparents.

"Nothing too terrible. We went boating the day before the competition, and we stayed out so long we got sunburned. I told Mom the engine stalled. Amie looked like a lobster." His reminiscent grin went tight. "Mom made her compete anyway. Just slathered her in more makeup. Amie got second runner-up."

"Seriously?"

"Scout's honor." He held up his fingers. "I offered to cut her hair but she nixed that, so we opted for the sunburn instead. I was never sure if she opted out of the haircut idea out of vanity or because Mom would have just bought a wig."

Preston studied the beautiful, eclectic woman sitting on the floor patiently piecing together a puzzle with Cody. She was focused on the child's wishes, on the child himself. She was an amazing woman in so many ways.

But he also could see how her upbringing would have left her with some hefty trust issues. Was her brother right to be worried? Because Preston was beginning to wonder if he had enough left inside him to give this woman who deserved—and would demand—one hundred percent.

Amie had felt jittery all evening watching Preston and her brother huddled together talking. What was Alex telling him? What did Preston want to know? She would find out soon enough now that Cody had calmed down enough to go to sleep. The puzzle had helped soothe him in the new locale. Nina was tucking him in now.

Preston had stepped onto the balcony to take an overseas business call. A breeze swept in through the open balcony door, carrying in his low and rumbly voice.

Amie rushed over to her brother as he straightened the puzzle on the coffee table, Monet's *Water Lily Pond*, a puzzle she'd gifted Cody with to connect through their love of art.

She knelt beside her brother. "Alex, be honest. Did Gran send you here to spy on me?"

He rocked back on his boot heels. "No, but that answers a big question. So Gran sent you on this trip for your inheritance test."

"I didn't say that," she hedged, crossing her arms.

"You don't have to."

She sank back onto her bottom, hugging her knees. "You tricked me."

"You fell for it…" He sat beside her and tugged her ponytail. "I just want to make sure you're okay. Preston is a shark. It's clear you two have something going on and I don't want you to get hurt."

Her heart hammered as she hugged her knees tighter. So it was that obvious. Their attraction was visible. But…that also meant Preston looked equally interested, enough to be noticed. And though Alex was playing the protective brother, the confirmation of Preston's interest gave her hope.

"If you think Preston's such a bad guy, why haven't you said something to Gran? You have influence with her."

"He's one helluva businessman and he will make the company successful, which is good for all of us. That doesn't mean I want him having anything to do with my sister."

She appreciated that he cared, but at the same time it bothered her that no one in this family seemed to think she could look after herself. Her pageant days might be long behind her, but people in her family were still so intent on making decisions for her. She didn't even want to consider her brother's reaction if he found out she was pregnant.

Deep breath. That wasn't important now. Not yet. One crisis, one task at a time.

Preston stepped back into the suite, closing the balcony door. He might be a shark, but damn, he took her breath away and set her senses on fire.

And time was running out fast to figure out how to deal with that.

* * *

Preston palmed Amie's back and led her into their suite, all too aware that her brother was so damn close. This whole dating ritual felt alien at forty-six years old. He wasn't a high schooler to sit on the sofa and be grilled by dad.

But Amie was tight with her family and there was no dodging all those concerned relatives. Truth be told, Alex's insights helped, even if he'd meant them as a warning.

Amie stepped into their suite and spun on her heels fast. "I can't wait another second to know. What were you and Alex talking about while I played with Cody?"

"Business." Images of Amie with pink tinged hair and a sunburn filled his mind, making her all the more approachable. Vulnerable.

Beautiful.

"That's all?" She perched her hands on her hips. "Somehow I'm having trouble believing you just talked about Diamonds in the Rough. My brother's known to be protective. It can't be coincidence that he showed up here now."

"Of course it's not a coincidence. He cares about you." Preston guided her deeper into the room, over to the balcony and their view of the Hudson River. He missed the outdoors. Needed the clarity. "But I can handle a worried relative."

"I hope so." She gripped the balcony railing, the NYC skyline lighting up the night, glittering like manufactured touchable stars. This was as romantic a setting as the park. Maybe the evening wasn't lost. Not yet. "I don't need any more conflict in my life right now."

A rogue thought struck him. "Did you tell him what happened between us?"

"No, of course not." Her eyes went wide with unmistakable horror. She shook her head. "I do *not* share that kind of information with him. That would be…creepy. But we're twins. There's an instinct between us. I'm certain he's here to check up on me. So I'll ask again. What did you two talk about?"

"Business—and yes, we talked about you." He skimmed his fingers over her high cheekbones and along her silky ponytail. "He shared stories about your pageant days and pranks you pulled to get out of attending some."

She angled closer, her feet tucked between his. "Why in the world would he do that?"

"I suspect he was lobbying to make sure I know you're more than a pretty face." He cupped the back of her neck. "But I already knew that."

"How so?" Her hand flattened against his chest, no hesitation.

There was a physical ease growing between them. It felt familiar. Comfortable. Natural.

"I work with you. You're damn smart." He tapped her temple. "Underestimating you would be a big mistake on anyone's part."

"Still—" she swayed even closer, bringing her lips inches away from his mouth "—it wasn't my brain that landed us in that coat closet together, since we hadn't even met."

Unable to resist her, all of her—body and brain—he sketched his mouth over hers. "Don't I know it."

Seven

His kiss sent Amie's already simmering passion into a full flame. She was so tired of fighting the attraction and had precious little time left to explore it before she told him about the baby. Tonight had been magical in a million ways, from their date in the park, to seeing him hang out with her brother and future nephew. In his own way, Preston fit. Or rather, she wanted him to fit.

But thinking that far ahead threatened to send her into a panic, so she focused on the present. On the warm stroke of his tongue with the taste of beer and pizza. The bold stroke of his hands along her spine, over her bottom to cup her hips and bring her closer. The press of his arousal sent a rush of power through her. This was real, happening again, not just another dream at night that left her feeling frustrated and aching.

He angled back to meet her eyes. "Are we headed for the bedroom?"

"Is that where you want to be?"

"You don't even have to ask that question."

"Neither do you. My only suggestion—" she looped her arms around his neck and she walked backward, sidestepping her cat "—let's begin in the shower."

His eyes flamed. "I like the way you think."

Their clothes fell away, leaving a trail of clothes as they walked into the Florentine-marble bathroom with an oversize steam rain shower and multiple body jets. He pulled a condom from his leather shaving kit, setting it inside the shower stall as he turned on the sprays, but stayed outside while the water heated.

"You're even more beautiful than I remember." He held her at arm's length, his eyes sweeping her curves and bringing tingles of awareness along her skin as surely as if he'd stroked her. "It's been driving me crazy the past two months thinking about that dark coat closet, wishing we had chosen a place with light and time. Hating like hell that it seemed we wouldn't get another chance."

She savored the breadth of his shoulders, the hard cut of muscles along his chest covered in dark hair. His narrow hips drew her eyes, her attention held by the thick arousal against his stomach.

She trailed her fingers down his chest, lower, his stomach muscles tensing visibly. "That night seems so surreal now."

With one finger, she traced the rigid length of him. His hard-on twitched against her touch and he groaned low in his throat.

His hazel eyes went steely with desire. "It happened."

"Believe me, I know." Her fingers wrapped around

the length of him. "I remember every detail, every moment."

He stepped closer, his hands cradling and caressing both her breasts. "This is going to be even better. I'm going to take my time."

She arched into his touch. "Promises?"

"I'm a man of my word." Dipping his head to kiss her again, he backed her into the shower.

No more reservations. She would have this and worry about the consequences tomorrow.

Preston backed Amie against the tile wall, taking the shower spray against his back. Her breasts filled his hands, the hardened peaks pressing into his palms as he stroked and caressed, then plucked with his thumbs... and mouth.

The spray pelted over their naked bodies, the beads of water mingling with sweat and need. Steam filled the shower stall, creating an even greater sense of privacy, a barrier between them and the outside world. For so long he'd ached for her, dreamed of having her totally. To learn every curve of her that he hadn't had time to explore before. She'd shut him out for so long. He wasn't a hundred percent sure why she'd changed her mind now, but he sure as hell wasn't turning his back on the chance to win her over.

He took a bar of soap in his hands, savoring the task in front of him. He applied all his focus to taking his time. Discovering all her secrets. All the places she liked to be touched best.

Steam surrounded them, a misty warm cloud along her wet skin while he worked up a lavender lather. She shifted from one foot to the other, drawing his eye toward long, slender legs slick with shower spray. Setting down the bar of soap, he reached for her shoulders and massaged the suds all over her.

Preston grinned hungrily, watching as her eyes drifted closed for a long moment, her muscles easing beneath his touch. He brushed kisses across her spiky, wet lashes while he slid his hands lower, kneading her high, full breasts until her knees seemed to give out from underneath her, making her sway. He pressed her to the tile wall with his hips, holding her upright.

Her breath caught as she reached for the soap, too, her fingers fumbling with it somewhere behind his back while he thumbed one dusky pink nipple to taut attention. She sighed in his ear, a throaty rush of breathless pleasure that only deepened when he took her in his mouth.

The soap fell from her hands and landed somewhere around his feet, but he couldn't stir himself to retrieve it. Not when her back arched the way it did right now, her whole body attuned to his slightest movement. Just like that first night when they'd danced. When they'd made love.

The chemistry at work was undeniable.

Still, she'd wanted a shower and he planned to deliver. So he forced himself back to hunt for shampoo.

Water saturated her hair, deepening the dark brown to ebony, and he squeezed the fruity-scented concoction into the locks, working it through, massaging her scalp while she hummed her pleasure. His hands slicked along the soaked strands, down her back to cup her bottom and bring her closer again. Skin to skin.

She sipped a kiss from him. "No more waiting. Now."

"And again in bed."

"Yes," she whispered, passing him the condom from the ledge.

He pressed inside her, moving, claiming.

The clamp of her around him was better than memories. The warmth of her body, the writhing of her hips was perfection. Bathroom lights and moonbeams streamed through the panes over her curves. No darkness. No shadows.

Just steam carrying the scent of soap and sex.

Her gasping breaths ramped, faster, her breasts pressing against him as her desire grew. He could feel it. Sense it. Her hand slapped against the glass wall as she braced herself, sliding down the condensation. Her head falling back, neck vulnerable.

As she unraveled with her orgasm, it was difficult to tell what was hotter—her or the steaming water. Finally, finally, he let himself go and thrust faster, deeper, wringing fresh sighs of pleasure from her as he found his own mind-shattering release.

And he knew he'd made the right decision. They would date, sleep together, work together, keeping it all civil and incredible.

They had all the time in the world.

Time was moving so fast. Knowing she was stuck in a twilight dream and unable to pull herself out, she rolled from side to side in the sheets, the Egyptian cotton sliding against her skin like Preston's touch. Her mind filled with an out-of-control reel, the past and present tangled, the night in the closet meshing with their encounter in the shower. Their clothes on from that night, but wet and plastered to their bodies. The peach-colored satin dress clung to her skin and shower spray slid from the brim of his Stetson.

She breathed in his scent, clean but spicy, too. Masculine. Heady. His touch warmed her where he touched her waist. Her hand.

The energy between them crackled like static through a rainstorm, crackling, dangerous along her skin. The music from that evening mingled with the percussion of the showerheads hitting the wall, their bodies, the floor. She breathed in and he breathed out. The writhing of their movements—dancing, making love, synced up effortlessly, her body responding to the slightest movement of his, shadowing his steps as she fell deeper into the spell of his hazel eyes.

The dim lighting of the coatroom and shower cast his face in shadows as she arched up into his kiss, his arms strong around her but loose enough she could leave if she wanted. But the last thing she wanted was to stop even though her mind shouted that she couldn't see his face, she didn't know who she was with. She needed to wipe away the water, let in the sunshine and see him. Know him.

Except pleasure pulsed through her at the angling of his mouth over hers, the touch of his tongue to hers. The kiss went deeper, faster, spiraling out of control. She pressed herself to the hard planes of his body. She lost herself in the kiss again, in the dream. In the feel and fantasy of this torrid dream that had her pressing her legs together in a delicious aching need for release.

Her breasts tingled and tightened into hard beads and her hands moved restlessly under the covers searching for him...but they were in the shower and the closet. And the hard length of his erection pressed against her stomach, a heavy pressure that burned right through the silky dress she'd worn.

She couldn't deny how much she wanted this. Him. Now.

He started to ease back and she stopped him, gripping his lapels. Slipping her hand into his tuxedo jacket, she let her fingers stroke across the muscled heat of his chest, water sloshing over them in her tangled mind. This was a man, the very best kind, powerful in body and mind.

His hands were back on her just as fast, roving, keeping the flame burning and—

Her breath was knocked from her.

She blinked awake, gasping for air as her cat stared back at her, perched on her chest. "Roscoe?"

The rascal must have jumped on her chest, worried over her restless dreams. She reached beside her and Preston still snoozed away, his breath heavy with sleep. She ran soft fingers on his forearm, unable to quiet her mind.

Eyes bleary, she stared at the digital clock on the nightstand: 1:30 a.m. A sigh escaped her lips. She needed to move. To think. To find clarity rather than thrash around in dreams she didn't understand.

Lifting Roscoe off and setting him on the floor, she carefully slipped out of the bed. He didn't stir. Neither did Preston. After the shower, they'd moved to the bed, slept, woken to make love again, taking their time, learning the nuances of each other. Then drifted off again. But still, she was restless.

From the floor, Amie grabbed Preston's T-shirt and put it on. It fell midthigh, like a short dress from her pageant days. But it smelled like Preston's musky cologne. It reassured her. Steadied her.

On tiptoe, she moved to the white chaise lounge across the room. The hand-stamped Venetian velvet made a gorgeous addition to the suite, and the kind of textural art that she loved best. She ran an appreciative hand along the pattern as she plopped down, clutching an oversize silk pillow to her stomach. Roscoe pattered over to her, tail straight up, shaking with excitement and affection. He jumped up, pawed at her until she lowered the pillow. He sat in her lap, purring, squinting his blue eyes at her. Roscoe always knew when she needed someone. When she needed comfort.

And damn. She needed that now more than ever.

Light from the city poured in through the window, allowing Amie to see Preston's figure in bed. He was a wonderful man. Caring. Confident. And more important, he seemed to believe in her. In her designs—at least the ones that she'd openly shared with him—and in her ability to make decisions.

Reaching for her stomach, Amie sighed deeply. There were too many unknowns.

For a moment, she allowed herself to think about what it might have been like if they had dated over the past couple of months. What they would be like. Would he be helping her pick out a nursery theme? Would he be offering names?

"Roscoe kitty, why is this so complicated?" she whispered. Roscoe simply looked up at her, purring still, and stretched his front paws to her belly. "We used a condom. I never sneak off into coat closets. And it's so hard to regret anything."

She scratched his head, wondering about what her

baby would look like. What life with her baby would look like. No, life with *their* baby. With his hazel eyes and her thick dark hair, chubby cheeks. Her heart went tight at the image of Preston smiling, rocking that child in his arms. If only life could be that simple, that easy. Had she blown her chance at it already?

Roscoe jumped from her lap and sprinted back to the bed, curling around Preston's head. Amie stayed for a moment on the chaise lounge before crawling back into bed, wanting to have Preston's warmth against her skin.

He stirred as she found her way back into his arms. He squeezed her tightly, and kissed the nape of her neck.

His breath was warm against her neck. If only things were different, less complicated. Somehow she would have to find a way to fix things between them. Wishing wasn't enough. She needed to act and soon.

Amie watched the clock for another few minutes before drifting to sleep.

After a catnap, Amie curled up against his side, the Egyptian cotton sheets tangled around their legs.

They were so good together it almost scared her, making her want to hesitate pushing for action and savor this just a while longer. It was just one night.

Preston stroked her bare shoulder while moving his toe under the sheet to entertain Roscoe. The cat pawed and pounced at the movement. "I'm disappointed your brother thinks I'm the bad guy."

"Well, you have cut a wide swath through the staff, firing off longtime employees we've grown to know and care about for years," she pointed out, tugging lightly at his chest hair.

He closed a hand around hers as Roscoe waddled slowly up the bed. "You mean, I saved the corporation."

"*Saved* is a strong word." She flattened her palm to his chest, his heartbeat steady and strong. "I would say you bolstered things."

"Semantics."

And likely why her grandmother had put him in charge instead of her.

Still, she frowned. "We lost a lot of talented people. Talented loyal people. I feel they deserved better from the company."

"It wouldn't help those talented and loyal people if the company started losing money. And that's what we were looking at. The employees don't thrive if the organization isn't thriving." He spoke with surprising passion, opening their blinds a bit with the remote control beside the bed, exposing an incredible view of the city lights in the middle of the night. "You know how many companies reorganize and then leave their people sweating it out for months afterward, worrying about their jobs? I happen to think it's kinder to circumvent the drama and the questions, making cuts as quickly and painlessly as possible."

"None of it was painless." Although she understood his point. She'd had friends who had been caught in corporate takeovers, worrying about their jobs for months while they navigated shifting seas at work.

"That's what severance packages are for." He shrugged. "I take personnel issues very, very seriously. I honestly believe the people are the backbone of any good company. That's not lip service. That's a fact. I happen to think it's one of the things your grandmother liked best about my philosophy when we first met."

"I believe you." She could see what had won over her grandmother. Preston might seem bottom line oriented. And he was. But he did care. "You just…look at things differently than me."

She wondered what he saw out that window overlooking the city right now. While she saw the lights and play of the moon over the river, he no doubt focused on other things.

"Different is not bad. Most artists are empathetic by nature. It's what makes them thrive in their work."

"Oh, really?" She grinned for a moment, realizing she'd never separate the man from the arrogance for long. But he was a smart man. And he'd obviously spent some time thinking about this kind of thing.

"Really."

They were quiet for a moment as she tried to process this new side of Preston. A side, she had to admit, appealed to her.

"I'm trying to see your take on things. My whole family has been more on edge recently because of Gran's cancer, so maybe not all the McNairs have given you a fair chance." That worry inside her—the fear that dogged her about the woman she loved most in the world—had been a large part of what had driven her into Preston's arms in the first place. "You're an outsider, so it will take us a while to trust you."

He lifted a strand of her hair. "Do *you* trust me?"

What a loaded question. She tugged the sheet up farther over her breasts, avoiding his eyes. "I trust you can lead Diamonds in the Rough."

"But you still wish it was in family hands."

Except then she wouldn't have met him and she wouldn't have this baby she loved more and more every day. Life was complicated. She opted for an honest answer—about the company. "I understand where my area of expertise falls at the company, but I still resent that I was not even considered for the CEO's position. I wasn't consulted about the choice. It stings."

"I'm sorry to hear that." He sat up, studying her face with those perceptive CEO eyes of his. "Your cousin didn't want the job. Did you?"

"I wanted to be considered." She sat up as well, hugging her knees to her chest.

"What makes you think you weren't?"

She rolled her eyes. "My family has never taken me seriously." Roscoe curled under her hand to be rubbed. "I'm the eccentric one, the airheaded beauty queen."

"You've proven you're at the top of your field at Diamonds in the Rough. Your more rustic designs are catching on like wildfire across the country and in England. You deserve to be proud of that. We all have a role to play."

She thought about the designs that weren't rustic. The ones he hadn't asked her much about. They might be all wrong for Diamonds in the Rough.

"I guess I just feel all the more need to prove there's no nepotism. My grandmother gives my father an office with a title and his name on the door."

"Your father's position is as a figurehead," he said matter-of-factly. "We know that. You contribute work, founding entire design lines. Sounds to me like you don't take yourself seriously."

She snapped back at the observation. One that was perhaps a little too astute for her peace of mind.

"Maybe you're right. And maybe you're not." She slid

off the bed, taking the sheet with her. "But I do know one thing for sure. I'm starving."

Seemed she was hungry all the time lately once the morning sickness passed. Her time was definitely running out to tell him about the baby. She'd rambled on about trust and yet she was lying to him in one of the worst ways possible.

They'd taken a big step here tonight. She just hoped the connection they'd made was enough to carry them through the news she had to tell him.

Preston leaned against the wet bar, facing the bay of windows looking out over one of the best views in Manhattan, but his eyes zeroed in on Amie. She perched on a leather bar stool wrapped in a sheet and eating a sliced pear, cheese and crackers from the cut-crystal dish as though she were a starved athlete. He'd learned to read people over the years, a survival skill in his job world. And he could see something huge weighed on her mind.

Nudging aside her empty plate and sliding it across the smooth granite countertop, she dabbed a napkin along the corners of her mouth with overplayed care. She folded the crisp linen napkin, set it down and pressed the crease nervously. "We need to talk."

Damn. He'd known something was off with her from the second she'd rolled out of bed. "Forget the speech about how we shouldn't have done this and it will never happen again. There's an attraction between us we've tried to deny and that hasn't worked. I say it's time to quit fighting it."

"Things aren't quite that simple." She pressed the napkin crease again and again.

"They can be. You can't deny what's between us any

longer, especially not after tonight." He picked up her hand and linked fingers, even the simple touch crackling the air with attraction.

"I hear you." She squeezed his hand, a sadness creeping across her face and catching in her eyes. "And in a different world things could have played out over the months."

"Different world?" He struggled to follow her words and for an astute CEO, he just wasn't getting it. But he wasn't letting go. "Is this because I head the company? It's not like I'm your boss any more than you're mine, since your family owns the business. That puts us on even footing."

She shook her head, tousled hair sliding over her cheek. "It's more complicated." She jerked her hand free and pushed her hair back with agitated fingers. "I've been looking for the right time—the right way— to tell you."

Tell him what? To go to hell? That she was seeing someone else? "Just say it."

She sat up straighter, her hands falling away from her head and settling to rest over her stomach. "I'm pregnant. And the baby is yours."

Eight

"You're pregnant?"

Preston's flat tone and stunned expression didn't give Amie much hope for an enthusiastic reception. She tucked the sheet more securely around her, wishing she'd chosen her timing better to make the announcement, when she felt less vulnerable from making love with him.

When she had on some clothes and he was wearing more than sweatpants low slung on his sexy narrow hips.

Arming herself with a bracing breath at least, she met his shocked gaze head-on. "Apparently the condom didn't work—welcome to the world of the two percent fail rate. And before you ask, I haven't been with anyone else in over six months, so I am absolutely certain the baby is yours."

He gave a rough nod. Swallowed visibly.

"I wasn't questioning. I trust your honesty." He thrust his hands through his tousled dark hair, the dusting of silver strands on the side a hint more pronounced in his stress. "I'm just...stunned."

She tipped her chin, trying to squelch the ache of disappointment in her heart that he hadn't...what? Just turned a cartwheel? Or hugged her and asked how she was feeling? Make her feel connected to him since they'd created this new life together? She knew better than to hope for those things. But that didn't stop the sting of hurt just the same.

"I don't expect anything from you. I'm able to support myself. I would hope for the baby's sake you would want to be a part of his or her life, but if you decide otherwise, I am not going to force you to pretend to care."

"Whoa, hold on. I didn't say I'm out of the picture." He started pacing restlessly around the luxury suite, the same way he did whenever he went into thinking mode in the boardroom. "I've had less than a minute to process this. I'm forty-six years old. This isn't the news I was expecting. I'm past that stage of my life."

She remembered his child who'd died and her heart softened. No doubt her baby would stir all the more difficult emotions for him. Yes, she understood that. Wished he would have confided more in her when she'd asked him about it. But he hadn't wanted that kind of intimacy between them.

His decision. And damn it, this wasn't easy for her, either. This baby was coming no matter what.

"Fine then." She clasped the sheet between her breasts and slid off the bar stool. "My baby. I'll take care of him or her and you can move on with the next stage of your life."

He clasped her elbow gently and stopped pacing. "Lower your defenses, Amie. This is my baby, too. And I may not be as young as most new parents, but I'm not Methuselah." He massaged her arm, his touch tender but his face still guarded. "I'm all in. Whatever you and the child need, I'm here for you both. I will be an active part of his or her life."

"Thanks for doing your duty," she said dryly, easing her arm away.

He sighed heavily. "Apparently I'm not expressing myself well."

"No, I'm hearing you just fine. And more than that, I can see in your face this news doesn't please you in the least." A knot started in her throat. Damn hormonal emotions.

"Are *you* happy?"

His question caught her off guard. She hadn't spent a lot of time thinking about her own emotions. She'd focused more on Preston's and her grandmother's reactions. "I'm nervous. But yes, there are days I have these images of what he or she will be like, and I'm happy."

"Pardon me for being human. You've had a while to process this surprise." He clasped her hand, holding firm. "Give me time to get over the shock of your being pregnant and I'll get to the happy part."

She eased a step closer, not quite ready to relent. "Well, forgive me if I'm skeptical."

Holding her gaze, he sat on the sofa, tugging her hand carefully until finally she sat on his lap and he held her close. They didn't speak and she let herself soak up the feeling of his arms around her. Maybe, just maybe, they could work things out in a way no one would be hurt or feel disappointed.

He rubbed his hands up and down her back. "Holy crap," he said slowly, realization lighting his eyes. "This is why you've been avoiding me lately."

"Ya think?" She pressed her cheek against his steady heartbeat.

"What about before you found out you were pregnant? Why did you give me the deep freeze then?"

Now, *that* surprised her. How could he be so clueless? "You honestly don't know?"

He shook his head. "Afraid not. Enlighten me."

"You were firing Diamonds in the Rough employees at the speed of light." She slid off his lap to sit beside him, the warm fuzzy moment over as indignation crept up her spine. "The poor staff was literally put on the island watching people voted off every day."

"You don't agree with the business decisions I made." He arched a dark eyebrow.

"Not all of them. No," she admitted.

"But you can't deny the company is thriving now. Those who are still working for us have jobs that are more secure than ever. With luck, we'll be able to hire more back."

Could that be true? Could she trust him? "When will that happen?"

"When the numbers speak."

She stifled disappointment at his typical double-talk answer. "Numbers don't talk. People do."

He spread his hands. "That's why you're the artist and I'm the CEO."

"And we're both now parents of this baby." She shot to her feet, feeling more hopeless than before that they could find a middle ground together. "I need to shower and rest. I just can't talk about this anymore."

Before she did something weak and vulnerable like curl up and cry against his chest. She dashed back to her bedroom and closed herself inside, alone with her cat and an even bigger tangle of emotions.

Maybe a better man would have gone after her.

Preston could not be that man. Not right now. Not when this news had ripped him raw.

Charging into his bedroom, he found his workout clothes and pulled on a clean T-shirt and running shorts. Socks. Shoes. He focused on the routine to keep himself from putting a hole through the nearest wall.

Amie pregnant. His daughter had died giving birth... The two events spun together. Clouded his mind. He needed to move.

He sprinted out of the suite and down fifty-two flights of stairs from the penthouse suite. He headed west on East Fifty-seventh Street and picked up his pace. Midtown was far quieter in the small hours of the morning. While it may be the city that never sleeps, 4:30 a.m. didn't attract the same kind of crowds. Cabs raced to the stoplights in the freedom of no traffic. Bars and clubs in unlikely places spilled music and colored lights out onto the sidewalk, making him dart around the occasional red velvet ropes set up on the street.

And Amie was pregnant.

Lungs burning, he hit Central Park before he realized where he'd been headed. Maybe not the wisest place to run after dark, but he pitied anyone who tried to mess with him. He'd love an excuse to throw a punch. Or ten. Anything to make this ache in his chest go away. The fire behind his eyes.

He'd lost his baby girl to a pregnancy. And now *Amie was pregnant.*

Tripping on a tree root as he darted off the sidewalk into the grass, he almost fell onto a homeless guy sleeping on a green painted bench, his face covered with newspaper.

"You okay, man?" the guy asked, a hand shoving aside last week's sports section as he stared up at Preston.

He nodded. Started running again.

Slower.

He spotted the pond up ahead and followed the path around it. Now and then a cab pulled onto one of the roads through the park, headlights flashing over him. A few street lamps lit his way. Nocturnal birds called out from the trees all around the pond, the conservancy efforts having made this portion of the park feel like being out in the country. Exactly what he needed.

Space. Air. Stillness.

Slowing his steps even more, he paced alongside the water's edge until he'd circled almost the whole way around. He hoped he'd sweat out the worst of the crushing fear for Amie. For his unborn child. He'd loved his daughter so much. Even during the years where he hadn't gotten to see Leslie much, he took joy and pride in knowing she was in the world. A small piece of him, but better than him. The very best of him.

Losing Leslie had cut so deep he'd barely stood it. There was the pain of losing her. Compounded by the fact that she'd died without getting to hold the infant she'd given up everything to have. And made even worse by the pain of knowing how much she hadn't wanted her own father in her life.

When Leslie had died, he'd taken time off from work—something he'd never done. Listless weeks he could hardly remember. But a company crisis had saved him. Forced him to dedicate everything he had to bending the corporate world to his will. There had been a grim satisfaction in that. And it had saved his sanity.

Now, he was going to face all that again. With Amie.

"You sure you're okay, man?" a gruff man's voice shouted to him from several yards away.

For a second, Preston figured voices in his head was just about right for the hell of the past hour. But then he saw a flash of newspaper waving at him from another bench surrounded by bushes and flowers. Lights illuminated the plantings—and the homeless man he'd almost tripped on before. The guy's grizzled beard and shaggy hair were so long they flowed over his T-shirt, but he held up both hands as if to show him he meant no harm.

"I'm good. Thanks. Just out for a jog."

But was it too much to ask to be alone with his thoughts?

"Sorry, dude," the scratchy voice rasped in the quiet of predawn when the sounds of night bugs were still more prominent than the rattle of diesel engines and squealing brakes in the distance. "Had a friend that came here to…er…end it all." The guy scratched his beard. "Got that same feeling when you sprinted past me."

"No problems here—" he started. But seeing the older guy's patches on a tattered jacket—military badges, Preston stopped with the bs answer. "Running off some old ghosts. But I'm…okay."

Scared spitless of having another child. Worried he might fail this baby the same way he'd let down Leslie… but he was going to find a way to get himself together.

Man up.

"Hard to keep 'em off your heels some days. I've had that kind, too." The man nodded thoughtfully, staring out at the pond.

Laughter nearby interrupted as a young couple stumbled past, sounding intoxicated as they held on to one another, doubled over with hilarity while the street lamps glinted off their matching face piercings.

Preston needed to get out of here. Get his butt back to the hotel and be there for Amie. For his child.

And the only way to do that? Wall off those emotions—the ghosts on his heels—and just focus on her. Getting through this. He was a man of honor and he would stand by her. His family.

His eyes burned even as he thought it.

Striding over to the older man, Preston took a deep breath.

"Thank you for your service." He held out his hand, knowing in his gut the man was a veteran fallen on hard times.

Sure enough, the guy grinned. A few teeth were missing. But his eyes held plenty of wisdom.

"You're welcome, son." His weathered grip was strong. "You might try surprising those ghosts sometime, by the way. Stop and turn instead of running. One of these days, you'll give them hell."

"I'll remember that." With a nod, Preston launched into a run, turning his feet back toward the luxury hotel that seemed a million miles away from this place.

He wasn't ready to battle any ghosts today. But for now he would count it a victory if he could talk to Amie about this child without breaking out in a cold sweat.

First, though? He needed to run faster, arrange with the concierge to find help for his veteran angel.

Then Preston would be ready to ask Amie to marry him.

The next day passed in a blur for Amie. She couldn't get a read on Preston. He'd been the perfect gentleman, but it was all so…perfect. Too perfect. He'd closed himself off from her in a way she couldn't explain but couldn't miss.

Technically, he'd done nothing wrong. They'd shared breakfast in the hotel dining room with Alex, Nina and Cody, then attended a Broadway matinee together. In fact, they'd spent the entire day together, leaving not one free moment alone to talk about the baby.

In another half hour, they would be leaving for the Diamonds in the Rough gala being held at the Waldorf Astoria. For now, Preston sprawled on the floor with Cody, playing with action figures from the children's performance they'd seen today. They were watching her future nephew while Alex and Nina got dressed. The sitter would be arriving soon—one of the camp counselors Cody had met and grown fond of. She was from home being flown in so Cody would have a familiar face to care for him.

Meanwhile, Preston looked too damn enticing playing in tuxedo pants and his shirt. No jacket or tie yet, just his suspenders and cummerbund. His broad hands moved the little lions, marching them over a mountain they'd built from throw pillows.

He was clearly at ease with children. But then, he'd told her he'd been a father and that his daughter had died. This new baby had to be bringing up old memories—good and painful ones. She should have thought of that before now.

The elevator door opened and Amie glanced over to see Nina walking through, wearing a floor-length black dress, simple other than the plunging neckline with a long yellow diamond pendant. Her red curly hair was upswept in a riot of spirals.

Amie rose from her chair and greeted Nina, grasping her hands. "You look amazing. I'm sorry if Alex caused you any trouble dragging you here to check up on me."

"A woman's never too old to play dress up. This is a fun break." She grinned, twirling, her silky dress swirling around her feet, a flash of gorgeous Jimmy Choo heels beneath. "And you, oh my, you do have a way of making a statement."

"This old rag?" Amie winked, but she couldn't deny she'd dressed to the nines, too. It was a kind of armor, a way to stabilize herself. The Grecian-style red dress was gathered on one shoulder, leaving the other bare, exposed. The gown was cinched on one hip with a brass medallion, a long slit up one leg. She hooked arms with her future sister-in-law and walked to the window seat where they could talk without Cody overhearing. And where she could gain a little distance from the appeal of Preston.

Amie sat in the window seat, cars below moving at the typical New York snail's pace. "How's Cody adjusting to your decision to stay at the ranch?"

"It's a love-hate thing." She smoothed her dress over her knees, her eyes lingering affectionately on her blond son. "He likes that we're going to live there now that Alex and I are engaged. He adores being around horses all the time. He gets along so well with Alex. Your brother is wonderful at getting through to him—and willing to learn more every day. He wants to go with me to interview new doctors and therapists for Cody. But it's all happened so fast, which makes it tough, because new routines upset Cody tremendously."

Amie chewed her lip before asking, "I hope you don't take this the wrong way, but why choose to come to New York now?"

"Alex is worried about you, and Cody was upset over him leaving, so we came along. Your brother says you haven't been yourself lately. I don't know you well enough to compare, but you do seem very...stressed."

Having someone to confide in felt good, but she didn't know how much she could tell her brother's fiancée, a woman none of them had known for very long at all, given the whirlwind romance. She needed to share the news with her grandmother first. And before she did that, she wanted to have things in order with Preston, to have a plan in place. Amie settled for a general—and still truthful—answer. "Gran's cancer progressing has us all worried."

"I can understand that. I mentioned the same to Alex, but he says it's different. He can sense it because of the twin connection."

Amie glanced down at her hands, anxiously twisting the four gold and topaz rings she'd chosen to go with her dress. "Things have been difficult at work."

Nina glanced at Preston, then back at her. "It's clear there's a chemistry, but I can see how that would be complicated. I'm here if you ever need someone to talk to."

She clasped Nina's hands, noticing they both wore one of the newest Diamonds in the Rough pieces, a sun and moon facing each other in silver and gold. "Thank you. I appreciate it and am sure I'll be taking you up on that soon."

"Just not today?"

Amie shook her head, smiling warmly. "Soon."

The elevator slid open again and her twin strode into the suite. Cody shot to his feet, carrying one of the lions to show him, chattering about the imaginary game he'd been playing with Preston.

Amie rose quickly. Too quickly. Her head started swimming and the room spun. Oh God. She reached for the wall, but her line of sight was narrowing to a pinpoint. Damn it, damn it, she was going to pass out.

Dimly, she realized Preston was rushing toward her. "Amie? Are you okay?" He caught her under the arms as her legs gave way. "Is it the baby?"

"Baby?" Alex barked.

"Baby?" Nina whispered.

"Baby, baby, baby," Cody chanted.

Preston swept her up as she fought back the dizziness. He settled her onto the sofa. "Amie?"

"I'm fine," she said, the room already stabilizing. "I just stood up too fast, and I could use some supper."

"Baby," Alex said again in a menacing tone, walking closer. "What the hell is going on here?"

Preston shot him a dagger glare. "Do not upset Amie."

Still, Alex walked closer. "My *sister* is pregnant?"

Nina gripped his arm. "Alex, I don't think this is the time or the place. When Amie's ready to talk, we can have a civil discussion. Maybe we should give them some space?"

Alex kept walking toward Preston as if Nina hadn't

spoken. "I'm asking you now. Is my sister pregnant and is the baby yours?"

Preston stood, his shoulders broad and braced, staring down her angry twin. "Yes, the baby is mine."

Oh God. Her twin was the quiet one in the family, but fiercely protective. So it was no surprise when he drew back his fist.

And punched Preston in the jaw.

Nine

Amie launched forward, shouting at her brother, tugging on his arm as he pulled back for another hit. "Alex, what the hell are you doing?"

Preston stumbled a step but stayed on his feet. His eyes went steely as he stared down Alex but pointed to her. "Amie, step out of the way." He zeroed in on Alex, that same alertness in Preston's body that she'd witnessed right before he took down a criminal on an LA street corner. "McNair, get yourself under control. Think about how this is upsetting your fiancée and Cody."

The young boy with autism was sitting on the floor with wide eyes, hugging his knees while rocking back and forth. Alex cursed softly, then kneeled beside his future stepson, all his focus shifting. "It's okay, Cody. I just lost my temper. Grown-ups do that sometimes. I'm sorry, buddy. Would you like to go back to our room with your mom?"

Cody nodded, standing, moving over to his mom. Nina cast a cautious look over her shoulder before shuttling her son out of the suite.

Alex took a deep breath, but his tense face said he wasn't backing down as he stared at Preston. "You knocked up my sister."

Amie gasped, stepping between them, hands raised. "Excuse me, but I am an adult. I make my own choices, and while I am expecting a baby, I take offense at the phrase 'knocked up.' I would also appreciate it if you didn't shout the pregnancy to the world. This is my business. I don't know why you're going all Cro-Magnon."

"Seriously? It doesn't take a math whiz to realize that since you haven't been around very long, the kid was conceived before you even had a chance to really get to know my—"

Preston growled, "Watch where you're headed with what you're saying. I let you have that first punch free and clear. But push me or say anything to Amie and I'm taking you down."

Alex's jaw jutted. "You can try."

Amie pressed a hand on each man's chest. "Stop. Both of you. You're both stressing me out and that's not good for the baby."

Alex's eyes narrowed, but she felt him ease a fraction. "Sister, you're manipulating me. I don't like that."

She patted her twin and looked into his familiar eyes, finally seeing more love than anger. "But I'm right. Thank you for your concern, but I'm okay. Go see Nina and Cody before you say something you'll regret. Your family needs you."

With a tight nod, Alex hugged her quickly. "Love you, Amie." He leveled a look toward Preston before backing away. "Be good to her or there will be hell to pay."

He stalked away and the elevator doors slid closed, leaving her alone with Preston. She reached to touch his jaw carefully along the red mark turning light purple. "Are you hurt?"

Her gaze ran all over him, taking in the powerful shoulders and chest. But his hands were impossibly gentle as they landed on her arms.

"It's nothing. I've taken worse. I just need to know you're all right."

Was she? Not really. Her heart pounded double time and she just wanted life to settle down. But there was nothing she could do about that. "I'm fine, and we have the party to attend."

His hand brushed her cheek, smoothing away a tendril that had slid out of place.

"We'll talk later," he promised.

A good thing or bad? She honestly didn't know. His expression was impossible to read. Cool despite his warm touch, and that worried her. Life had been so much simpler when they were in a coat closet and shower.

Five hours later, Amie put together an ice pack from the limo minifridge. The gala had been a success from a business standpoint, with the displays echoed by edible-desert versions the guests feasted on with relish. But the event hadn't been nearly as pleasant from a personal perspective. Nina and Alex had opted to stay at the hotel with Cody. And Preston had been distant and remote but utterly in control. He'd done his job impeccably. He'd been a consummate gentleman and efficient CEO as he chose a few key people to speak with, applying just the right amount of charisma on a night that called for a personal touch. He'd even laughed off questions about his bruised face, saying he'd run into a street light while jogging.

But even so, there was still no sign of the tender lover, the man she'd started to think she could have a relationship with. He'd shut down on her ever since the baby news. She needed to get past that polite wall again, for her child's sake—and yes, for her own peace of mind.

Preston sat in the plush leather limo seat, collar unbuttoned, looking handsomely disheveled. Clutching the ice pack, Amie inched next to him, closing the space between them.

She pressed the bag of ice against his jaw and the light purple bruise. "I'm so sorry my brother hit you."

"He loves you. He didn't break anything. It's okay." He seemed to have turned the explosive moment into a simple math equation, reducing it to a balance sheet with a measurable figure. Always a businessman. Calculating.

"It's not okay. It was awful." She shivered thinking of the moment her brother had taken a swing at Preston. She dabbed the ice pack along his jaw while the limo slowed for a red light. "Can we at least talk honestly here instead of this cool and distant approach? If you've decided you're not okay with the baby, after all, just tell me. I can't take living in limbo." Her heart slammed as she waited for his response. In what way had he decided to coolly solve this complicated equation?

"I've already told you I'm going to be a part of the

baby's life." He smiled, then winced, his jaw clearly sore. "I want to be in your life, too."

"I hear the words, but your eyes are not the same." He was still closed off. She could see it in the way he refused to really look at her. "Something's wrong and you're not telling me. I know this has happened fast, but we don't have the luxury of unlimited time. Not with a baby on the way."

He tugged the ice pack from her hand and tossed it aside in irritation. "I'm giving you everything I have."

"*Giving* me?"

"Everything I have. Yes," he said, his voice clipped. "This is all there is."

"What does that mean?" she pressed, not even sure what she was searching for from him, but certainly not this. "You either want to be with me or you don't."

His jaw flexed, his stormy eyes darting back and forth for an instant before he finally exhaled, his head falling back against the leather seat. "I told you I had a daughter and that she died. This new baby has brought up a lot of memories. Tough memories to deal with."

Her heart softened. She'd suspected this, but to hear him say it—it took the fight right out of her. She smoothed a hand down his arm, the fine fabric of his tuxedo warm from his body. "Tell me, Preston, please. Let me know what's going on inside you. Your daughter is my baby's sister. I want to know—I need to know."

The car started forward, the tinted windows muting the headlights and street lamps on Park Avenue, past an older residential section of the city. She saw the lights reflect on Preston's face while he seemed to debate what to tell her.

Finally, his throat moved in a long hard swallow. "Leslie was just eighteen when she died."

So young, so tragic. And at the same time, Amie realized he'd lived a whole other life before walking into hers just two months ago. He'd told her more than once he considered himself too old for her. She didn't agree but could see right now why he felt that way.

Hoping he wouldn't close her out again, she kept rubbing his arm. "You said she had an accident. I can only imagine how that must still hurt." Her voice was soft, gentle. She brimmed with the ache to be someone he could trust. The car slowed to a stop again, and this time, the flood of red brake lights nearby created a crimson glow inside the limo.

He shook his head. "I don't think anyone gets over losing a child. And the fact that Leslie's death was preventable eats me alive every day."

Preventable? He'd said it was an accident, but clearly he'd said so to brush people—her—off. But not tonight. They'd moved past that. They were tied together for life through this baby. "What happened?"

"It's a long story without a simple answer." He turned his head toward her, his eyes full of pain.

"I'm listening." A sympathetic, encouraging smile brushed her lips as she squeezed his hand.

"Her mother and I split when Leslie was just finishing elementary school. They both hated me for leaving." He winced over that part, the pain flashing again. "And Leslie hated her mother for staying. There was no reasoning with her. She became an out-of-control teenager. Some say she would have been that way regardless, but I worked too much and missed so many of my scheduled visitations. Time I can never get back." He rested his elbow on his knee, dropping his head into his hands.

"I'm sure you did the best you could." She rubbed circles along his broad back, their car stuck in gridlock just a few minutes from their hotel.

She suspected they wouldn't be moving anywhere for a while. And this time, she had no intention of leaving the limo.

"How can you be so certain?" he asked softly.

"You're a perfectionist. You hold yourself to a standard so high most would be crushed."

His laugh was bitter as he sat up again. "That's my business persona. My parenting skills were sorely lacking. I thought by giving her nice things I didn't have as a kid, I was being a good dad. Trust me, I see how screwed up that is now."

"How did she die?" she pressed again.

"She ran away from home at seventeen with her loser boyfriend," he said, the bitterness in his voice unmistakable. "She got pregnant, didn't get proper prenatal care. She died and the baby didn't make it. Something called placenta previa. She went into premature labor and by the time she got to the ER…it was too late."

Amie stifled a gasp, the story so much worse than she'd expected, so painful. So terribly tragic. "No wonder you're worried about becoming a parent again."

Losing his daughter through a pregnancy added a whole other layer to his emotions where Amie's baby was concerned. It made sense now that he'd looked so rattled when she'd told him. The lines of worry that etched in his jaw all evening made more sense. Seemed more reasonable.

"It's tough not to worry about your health and the

baby. It's all I can think about sometimes, all the things that could go wrong." His eyes sheened over. He stared out in front of them.

An ambulance honked nearby, lights flashing while it went up on the sidewalk to get through the jam.

"I'm taking care of myself and am absolutely getting the best care available." Clasping his hands in both of hers, she pressed his to her stomach.

He froze again, his palm broad and warm through her silky dress. Preston stared at her stomach before meeting her gaze. His face was contorted with a sadness she could not quite comprehend. "That's not what's scaring me most."

"What then?"

"I'm scared as hell of loving another child and screwing up—" his voice came out ragged, tortured "—of having my soul ripped out if something happens to him or her. I can't go through that again. My heart died that day, Amie. I don't think I have anything left to give the two of you and that's so damn unfair."

He squeezed his eyes closed, no tears escaping, and she knew that just meant he kept them bottled up inside with all that pain and misplaced guilt.

"Preston? Preston," she said again until he looked at her. "You seem to care a lot more than you like to let on. I can see it in your eyes."

"You're seeing what you want to see."

"Trust me—" she cupped his face and couldn't help but notice he left his hands on her stomach where their baby grew "—I may be an artist, but I'm the most starkly realistic one in the family."

She was far more practical than people gave her credit for, a side effect of having her every move scrutinized by a stage mother—a mother she did not intend to emulate.

Her thoughts were cut short by the soft chime of a bell that preceded an announcement from the driver.

"Excuse me, Mr. Armstrong. My apologies for choosing this route, sir. There's an overturned bus ahead. Looks like we may be stuck here for a while."

Preston hit the speaker button. "Not a problem. Thank you for the update."

Releasing the light on the communications panel, he stared at her in the dim light of the luxury car, his eyes bright with inscrutable emotions slowly shifting to…hunger.

It was her only warning before he leaned closer and pressed his mouth to hers, kissing her. Not a quick kiss. But the kind that promised more.

So much more.

The old hurt and anger roiled inside him. But this time, instead of running it out, he had Amie's hands on him. Amie's soft voice in his ear and slender body shifting beside him on the limo seat. It was tough to resist her on a good day. And this day? The last twenty-four hours had shredded him.

All the emotions surged and shifted into one inescapable need.

He kissed her hard. Deep. But he made sure to be gentle with his hands and his body. He skimmed a touch along her bare shoulders, feeling her shiver and tremble. She was exquisitely sensitive. He'd been an ass not to see the signs of her pregnancy earlier. But now? It seemed written all over her body.

In the way she quivered against him when he did

something small, like nip her ear the way he did now.
Or when he licked his way down her neck and her skin
broke out in goose bumps.

The limo windows were the blackout kind. No one
could see in. The partition window was secured, he'd
double-checked it on the communications panel. Doors
locked. Traffic jam keeping them right here for a long
time.

So he didn't quit kissing her. He laid her back on the
seat and stretched out alongside her, never breaking his
kiss down her chest to the swell of her breast. More
delicious evidence of her pregnancy. He'd just thought
her curves were even more lush than he'd remembered
from that first wild night together. But now, he cupped
the weight of them in both hands, savoring the way she
felt almost as much as he liked hearing her breath catch.

Dipping his head to the valley between her breasts,
he nudged aside the pin on her red Grecian gown, es-
sentially undoing all her clothes with just one touch.
A red lace bra molded to her curves, but a flick of the
front hinge had that falling away, too.

Impatient as hell, needing to lose himself in her—
in this—he circled one tight crest with his tongue even
as he slid his hand up her thigh. She arched and sighed
beneath his touch, totally on board with this plan. He
nudged aside the lace panties she wore, feeling her
warmth right through the thin fabric.

"Amie." He said her name so she would open her
eyes.

Put all that brilliant blue focus on him as he touched
her. She was a beautiful woman, but damn...so much
more than that. He watched her lips part as he slid a

touch inside her. Her eyes fell closed again. Her thighs clamping tight to his hand to hold the touch there.

As if he was going anywhere.

He covered her mouth with his again, working her with his hand until he felt the rhythm of her sighs and throaty little hums of pleasure. Finding the pace she liked best, he took her higher. Teased her. Tempted her.

He wanted to draw it out. To make it last, but she had her own ideas. She captured his wrist in her hand. Held him right where she wanted him most.

"You like that?" He repeated the circling motion, bending to draw on one breast. Then the other. "I like it, too."

"More," she demanded, voice rasping, her blue gaze landing on his.

Complying, he drove her right where she needed to be, her cries of completion sweet music in his ear as she found her release.

Another day, he might have given her a little time to recover herself. Or taken her to that peak a second time while she was so delectably willing in his arms. But just then, that dark, hungry need returned, his emotions churning to the surface. Reminding him how damn much he needed her.

"Preston?" She smoothed her fingers along his shoulder, making him realize he hadn't even removed his jacket.

He ditched it now, sitting up on the seat.

"I'm going to bring you up here, sweetheart," he crooned as he peeled away her panties and then lifted her. Gently. Carefully. He moved her onto his lap so she straddled him.

Her thighs splayed over his, remnants of her red silk

gown still clung to her thighs and waist. She unfastened his belt and tuxedo pants, freeing him from his boxers. He watched her, her dark hair mostly falling around her shoulders, the updo sacrificed to their frenzy.

She stroked him, fingers cool and nimble as she guided him closer to where she wanted him.

Grasping her hips, he lifted her high and then eased her down. Down. Deeper.

Perfect.

Everything else fell away. Her slick heat surrounded him, holding him tight. Her hands fell to his chest where she steadied herself. She brushed a kiss along his cheek, urging him on. Telling him what she needed in a way that only fueled him up. His hands molded to her waist. Smoothed up to her breasts.

He had a lot of other ideas for his hands, too. But she gripped his wrists again. Pinned them to the limo seat on either side of his head as if she had him captive. She arched an eyebrow at him. Teasing.

But then things got crazy. She swayed her hips in a dance that about turned him inside out. Lifting up on her knees, she found a rhythm she liked and took them both higher. Faster. And he let her. Not thinking right now—great idea. He took everything she was giving him.

When her grip slipped on his wrists, though, he sensed she was close. He held her waist, taking over, pushing them the rest of the way. Her release squeezed him hard, spurring his own. With no condom between them, the pleasure seemed to last all the longer, the pregnancy issue moot at this point, and hell if that didn't feel…so good.

Wrung dry, he shuddered a deep sigh and folded her

against him. Holding her. Kissing her bare shoulder as a silk strand of her dark hair teased his nose. He spanned a hand along her back, rubbing slow circles while he tried to find his breath again.

He couldn't bear to think about the past anymore. And thinking about the future raked him raw with fears as well. Walling off the past didn't mean he had to wall himself off from the future. He just wanted to lose himself in the present, with Amie.

"I'm sorry for being distant earlier today. I just needed some time to myself to think."

"I know." She shifted against him, resituating herself so she sat beside him, her head tucked against his chest. Her hand covering his heart. "I've had more time to process this than you, and even for me I feel like I can't wrap my head around it. Everything is changing so fast. Both with my grandmother and the baby."

"Let me help you. Your whole family works together and depends on each other. We're tied now through this child, so let me into that circle." He hoped it was the right time for this—the most important pitch of his life.

But it needed to happen and he couldn't fail. She meant too much to him.

"What do you have in mind?" She lifted her head, eyeing him as the limousine finally inched forward.

Preston took her hands in his and hoped his eyes didn't betray his fears. The time had come to tear down some walls and start letting her in if they would stand a chance at building a future together.

"Let's get married."

Ten

"**M**arried?" Shock chilled Amie to the core, the leather crackling under her as she inched back to look into Preston's eyes. She'd expected him to pursue her because of the baby. But she hadn't expected this. It felt too forced, too sudden. Too rehearsed. "You have got to be kidding."

"I'm completely serious." His voice was steady, eyes trained on her face.

Amie shook her head in disbelief. "We've only known each other a couple of months. That's a huge leap to take just because I'm pregnant."

She knew he was only proposing because of the baby, and maybe even to secure things at the company, too. Old insecurities flamed to life inside her and she couldn't shut them down no matter how much she wanted to believe their connection was special. That given more time, they could have gotten to this place on their own. And maybe they would have. But now there was no way to separate fact from fiction.

Preston reached for her hand. He ran his thumb over her knuckles. His face etched calmness. Stability. Reminding her of his boardroom demeanor, where he focused on the goal and calmly maneuvered his way there. Her gut wrenched.

"Sure, it hasn't been long, but you can't deny we have something good going here. We have an attraction beyond anything I've experienced. We get along now that you're not icing me out at the office. We work well together. I know we can build a future together for ourselves and this baby."

A part of her heart leaped at the idea of being married to Preston. He was a good man. Protective. Confident. Sexy as hell. But she wouldn't settle for being his end goal just because he felt as if he should marry her. Ever since her pageant days, people had taken it upon themselves to judge what was best for her. To tell her what she needed, what she desired. For so long, she hadn't cared about the outcome of the pageants, so she let herself be told what to wear, what act to perform and how to answer interview questions.

Was Preston just like that, deciding this was the most logical outcome to their problem? Deciding what was best for her? She couldn't allow herself to take the path of least resistance just because it was simple. And the man in question was irresistibly appealing. She owed her baby better.

She wanted to trust what he said, but she needed more from him. Was it so wrong to want him to want her, child and company aside? "We don't have to decide now. We have a few months to think this through."

"I take it that's a no." He still held her hand, but his grip loosened.

"I just want us to make the right choices—for ourselves and the baby. We still have time with the Atlanta event before we have to face the family at home…"

"Family." He slumped back in the seat, dropping her hand. Running his fingers through his hair, he let out a pent-up sigh. "I hadn't thought about all of them."

"And your parents. Do you have other family?"

He shook his head. "Not since Leslie died."

"Do you still communicate with your ex-wife?" Amie knew so little about his life before the company. Before her. They were tied together through this child. And if he was going to make hasty decisions, she would make sure she balanced that with all the important angles he was overlooking.

He blinked in surprise but answered quickly. "Not often or regularly. Last I heard, she and her new husband moved to Georgia. They adopted two children, siblings that had been orphaned."

"And you're okay with her remarrying and having kids?" Her breath caught in her throat, heart pounding as she asked the question.

"Of course I'm all right with that. I want her to move on and have a future."

Yet he hadn't moved on for himself. Or was that what he was trying to do now? So tough to tell when she didn't know much about him or his past. "What was your daughter like when she was little?"

"Feisty, independent." He laughed out the words. Preston's gaze seemed to turn inward. Thoughtful.

Amie knew in that moment how much he had loved his daughter.

"Sounds like her father." Amie grinned at him, placing her hand on his knee, leaning closer. This was a hard subject for him. She wanted to make sure he didn't close up on her. And that he knew she was here to listen.

"Except for the pigtails."

"Now, that's an image." Her smile widened. "What color was her hair?"

"Dark, like mine. She was an active child. She walked early, loved her trike. I bought her a pony, a fat little bay mare from Chincoteague, Virginia. She loved the books about the ponies from that island. It seemed suited that she had a formerly wild pony as her own." He hung his head. "My ex said I used gifts to make up for lack of time."

"That could be true, but it also sounds like you knew her and her wishes. Time together doesn't always translate to a quality relationship anyway. My parents spent plenty of time with me and never had a clue what I wanted to do or what gifts I may have preferred."

"I appreciate you trying to let me off the hook. But I made mistakes. I have to live with that. I'm going to do my best not to make the same mistakes with this child." Genuine promises shone in his eyes.

Amie desperately wanted to believe that's what she was seeing. "My baby's lucky to have you as a father."

"Our baby," he softly corrected her.

"Right, I'm still adjusting, too." She was fidgety. Her fingertips smoothed back her hair, but nothing was out of place—unlike her insides that were a mess.

"I want to be more than the dad. I want to be there. With you and the baby."

"I told you, I need more time to think about the proposal." Her voice edged with more steel than she intended. While she was starting to have a clearer picture of Preston the father, the image of Preston the husband was still elusive. And she would not settle. She needed someone that genuinely wanted her.

Preston considered her words. Amie could see him recalculating. "Well then, how about we move in together and if we decide to get married one day, we can head to the courthouse. Let me at least be there to help you through the pregnancy day by day."

"I have a houseful of servants." She was thinking practically, suspecting he was doing the same.

"Good. Because I suck at doing laundry." He offered her a causal grin. "So is that a yes to moving in together?"

She studied his face, trying to get a read on him. If only she had spent the past two months getting to know him. She might have been able to tell something from the light in his hazel eyes. "Let's enjoy the next couple of days and decide after the Atlanta show so we have a plan in place when we talk to our families."

He studied her at length as if he intended to press, then nodded. "I can live with that." He slid his hand behind her neck, fingers massaging her scalp. "In the meantime, I intend to make the most of every second to fully and completely seduce you."

She looped her arms around his neck. "Maybe I intend to seduce you first."

Preston lint rolled cat fur from his tuxedo, making sure not a stray hair was in sight. Tonight was important. And not just for the gala. It meant more than selling jewelry and making this line succeed.

He needed to sell Amie on the idea of them. She hadn't outright rejected the idea of them together, but she wouldn't commit to the proposal. He could see hesitation and questions in her eyes.

If she would just say yes, he could do away with so many of those fears. He had meant what he said about wanting to be there for their baby. For her. He wanted to do this right.

There had to be a way to convince her that he was serious about her. That he wanted to pamper and take care of her and their unborn child.

She was an amazing woman. Independent. And she was smarter than she gave herself credit for. Her artistic instincts were brilliant and he hated that she couldn't see how much she was worth to the company. To him in particular.

Amie riled him, made him want to try harder. There was something in the way she carried herself, in her sarcasm and eclectic flair that drew him in. No one but Amie would ever consider taking an elderly and sickly cat on a business trip just to ensure proper care was administered. Her heart was so big. He wanted a place in it.

He'd been racking his brain on how to show her he cared. How to prove to her practical nature that he cared. Or maybe…

He stopped the mindless brushing of his tuxedo jacket and put the lint roller down on the floor for Roscoe to play with—the cat was a primo escape artist, sneaking out of Amie's room. Maybe he didn't need to show her he cared so much as show her that he believed in her.

Hadn't she said that no one in her family took her seriously? That she wasn't even asked about heading the company? A plan came together in his mind as he thought of ways he could show her just how much he valued her. She might think his efforts to prove his faith in her were just corporate maneuvering. And— he had to admit—the plan he had in mind was straight out of his boardroom toolbox. But for a woman who felt as if she hadn't been taken seriously in the business world, it might help her to understand that he saw her differently.

That he recognized more than her legendary beauty or her obvious wealth. He respected the hell out of her.

Picking up his cell phone, he tapped the lint roller into motion for Roscoe again while trotting out some instructions to his personal assistant to get the ball rolling on his idea.

A few moments later, his work was interrupted when the door to his suite clicked open and Amie stepped through the threshold. She was radiant.

Yes, beautiful, but so much more.

He would convince her to marry him, one way or another. He had to.

Amie was used to working close to home, which meant she wore casual business attire some days and ranch clothes on others. All these galas so close together gave her flashbacks to her pageant days. Except at least she got to choose her own clothes now. No more traditional stage garb like the kind her mother insisted on as her "manager."

Now she could let her creative impulses run free. And yes, she had to confess, she enjoyed watching the heat flame in Preston's eyes every time she made an entrance.

Since she'd pushed the edgy boundaries before, she went for a simpler look tonight, a fitted gold lace dress that flared around her feet. Her hair was slicked back into a tight bun. Simple, classic cat eyeliner and nude lips. Dangling hammered-flat gold earrings and multiple wide bracelets were engraved with her favorite quotes from her favorite poets. All the words of encouragement and perseverance were strung around her wrists. There to remind her to breathe.

She walked down the grand winding staircase at the Saint Regis Hotel where they were staying and holding the event. No getting trapped in a limo together tonight.

Her body heated at the memory of making love in the backseat. And continuing through the night when they'd returned to their hotel. The trip on the private jet had been too quick and full of business for any deep conversation, but that marriage proposal still hung in the air between them.

Could she really just move in with him and see what happened over the next few months? She wished she knew the answer or saw some kind of sign. She felt adrift with nowhere to turn. Her mother wouldn't be a help at all. Her brother had made his adversarial position clear. And she didn't want to burden her grandmother.

Her fingers clenched around Preston's elbow as they reached the bottom of the staircase, noise from the jewelry show already drifting down the hall along with music from a string quartet.

Preston glanced at her. "Are you feeling all right? Tired? Or dizzy?"

"I'm feeling fine," she said quickly. Of course, he'd meant the baby, not the proposal or her feelings. "I'm taking my prenatal vitamins religiously. I promise."

"Just making sure you aren't overdoing it. It's been a hectic week." He patted her arm. "Let's get to the party and find some food."

Okay, more pregnancy concerns, but it was thoughtful and she was starving. She spotted a waiter heading into the ballroom with a silver platter of persimmon pear caprese toast. Another with what looked like goat cheese and beets. Her mouth watered.

"Definitely food. Sooner rather than later."

He smiled down at her with such light in his eyes she felt hope flutter to life inside her. Maybe, just maybe, they could be happy, sharing great sex and working hard to build a future together. They were both driven people. If they set their minds to this…

He dropped a quick kiss on her lips before escorting her into the ballroom teeming with jewelry displays on models strategically seated and standing on small themed stages throughout the room. As songs changed, they changed jewels from the display cases beside them. More than just a runway event, they'd created an interactive jewelry fashion show to play throughout the evening. She was quite proud of the execution of this idea, the thematic podiums echoing the various Diamonds in the Rough lines.

She snagged an appetizer from a passing waiter. Cheese truffle with chives. She could have eaten a dozen. Her mouth full, she looked around the domed space, searching for the contacts she needed to make.

Taking her time to work the room, she sampled her way along the perimeter.

Preston went still beside her, stopping her short of her goal of a mini lobster soufflé.

"What's wrong?" She followed his gaze and realized his attention was focused on a lovely blonde in a pale blue dress walking toward them on the arm of a distinguished-looking man in a conservative tux. "Preston?"

"Amie…" He paused, his forehead furrowing. "I'm not sure how to tell you this or why she's here, but—"

The woman stopped directly in front of them. "Hello, Preston, it's been too long, but you're looking good." She extended her hand to Amie. "I'm Dara West. I used to be married to Preston."

After an awkward introduction to Amie, Preston cornered his ex-wife by the triple chocolate fondue fountains surrounded by fruit and small delicacies. She always had adored her sweets. That had gotten him out of trouble more times than he could count. He'd known they were through the day she'd thrown a box of her favorite Godiva's exclusive G Collection chocolates at his head after he missed Leslie's fourth-grade dance recital because he'd worked late. No good excuse.

"Dara, what the hell are you doing here?"

"I do keep up with your life thanks to the internet and an occasional Google search. I saw photos of you and Amie in the social pages. I know you, and I could see there's a connection between the two of you. I was curious." She picked up a glass of champagne from a passing waiter.

"And your husband doesn't mind?" Preston raised his eyebrows in disbelief.

"Bradley and I are secure. Solid. Besides, coming here gave us an excuse for a weekend away together. Mom and Dad are thrilled to watch the kids."

"The kids are—" he swallowed hard, thinking back to the photograph she'd sent—a family, a complete family "—beautiful. Thank you for the Christmas card."

"I'm happy..." Dara's voice trailed, became leaden. She shook her head. "Well, there was a time I didn't think that happy was possible. But I love Bradley, unconditionally, and I've worked hard to find happiness again after what you and I went through. I keep hoping you'll find a way to be happy, too."

Leslie's death had shredded Dara as deeply as it had hurt him. He knew that.

"So here you are, checking up on my happy meter." Preston's arms crossed over his chest.

"Checking up to make sure Amie McNair is worthy of you." She gestured with her champagne flute to Amie, who was standing chatting with a potential client. She took Preston's breath away with her understated charm and love for the company, for people.

He threw back his head and laughed. "You are something else, Dara. But thank you. I can take care of myself. Truth be told, Amie's too good for me."

"Spoken like the gentleman you've always been."

"Not always." Preston's eyes darkened, muscles tensing. He had spent years ignoring and burying his past. His ex. His dead child and premature grandchild. These past few days had brought every painful memory lurching back to the surface. "I'm sorry I let you and Leslie down. Sorrier than you'll ever know."

"Casting blame takes away from thoughts of remembering her. I want to remember her and smile." She looked thoughtfully at him. And she seemed to be at peace.

"How did you do it?"

"Do what?" Dara's green eyes looked back inquisitively.

Preston let out a long-held breath. He shrugged his shoulders. "Get up the guts to have another child in your life?"

She nodded her head in understanding. "I have a mother's love to give and nowhere to pour it. There are children who need that love."

"You're a good woman. I was an idiot to let you get away."

"You aren't about to hit on me, are you?"

"Our time passed before Leslie died. I know that." The weight of the past threatened to drag him under. He needed to lighten the mood. Fast. "Besides, your husband would kick my ass."

"He would try. But we both know you could take him." She winked at him, tossing her blond hair over her shoulder with a dramatic flick of the hand.

"Flattery? You surprise me." He laughed. The conversation was easier than he could have ever imagined, than he felt he deserved.

"I've realized our breakup wasn't entirely your fault. I had my part in how things went south between us."

"That's kind of you to say, but I know—"

"Stop. You don't have to protect me from myself. I take responsibility for my own actions. That's a part of how I was able to move forward and enjoy my future." Dara smiled at him.

If she could move on, could he? Could he stop running from those old ghosts?

He sighed, the words falling out before he could weigh the wisdom or why of speaking them. "Amie is pregnant. The baby's mine."

Her eyes flashed with only an instant's surprise, then total joy. "Congratulations. That's wonderful news."

"It is." Pain crept into his words.

"Then why aren't you smiling?"

"Amie won't marry me. I'm having to work my ass off just to get her to agree to let us move in together."

"She doesn't love you in return?"

He scratched the back of his neck. "We, uh, didn't talk about love."

Dara rolled her eyes. "She won't marry a man who doesn't love her, who only proposed to her because she's pregnant. Hmm…" She tapped her chin in mock thought. "I wonder why she said no. That would have been enough to sell me."

Sarcasm dripped. And yet, the theatrical delivery helped him get the message. Sometimes he needed things spelled out for him.

Damn. How could he be so successful in the business world and such a screwup in the relationship department? Of course Amie wanted more from him. How had he overlooked that? "Okay, I hear you. And by the way, you're funnier than I remember."

"And I'm hoping you still remember how to be romantic. There was a time you were quite good at that. You do love her, don't you?"

"This is not the way I saw this conversation going," Preston admitted.

She raised an inquisitive brow at him. "But you're not denying it."

"Because I can't." Realization bubbled in his stomach.

She rolled her eyes, tilting her glass back to Amie. "Well, don't tell me. Tell her."

Eleven

Amie kept her cat in her lap on the flight back to Fort
Worth, needing the comfort of stroking Roscoe. The
rhythm of Roscoe's purring was the only thing anchoring her. The last week had left her raw. Vulnerable. She
had spanned a year's worth of emotions over the course
of a few days. How could it have only been a week since
her grandmother gave her orders to travel with Preston,
to make peace with him for the future of the company?

She felt anything but peaceful after seeing the way
Preston greeted his ex-wife. It was obvious he had feelings for her. It didn't matter that Dara had moved on
with a new family. Amie hadn't been able to take her
eyes off Preston with his former wife at the party in Atlanta, mesmerized by the emotions she saw broadcast
through his hazel eyes.

Emotions she'd never seen for her.

She'd hardly slept afterward, her stomach churning all night, knowing that Preston didn't care for her that way. Knowing she didn't have a fraction of his heart. His offer to stay, to marry her, was not out of desire or longing for her.

Roscoe nudged closer, standing to make his feline presence felt. She brushed her fingers behind his ear, doing her best to keep herself from shedding tears on the flight home. Instead, Amie concentrated hard on Roscoe's purring. She could only imagine the turmoil that would erupt over her news, especially with the memory of Alex's reaction weighing on her heart.

She needed to do what she could to control the family response. Which meant talking to Preston. And she wasn't ready to face more questions about marriage or moving in. She needed time and space to think.

Stroking the senior Siamese, fur soft under her fingers, she hoped it was a good time to broach the topic. On her terms. "Now that Alex and Nina know, it's only a matter of time before word gets out."

Preston stretched out his long legs, crossing his boots at the ankles, wearing faded jeans with his suit jacket now that the galas were done. "Do you think they would talk, even if you asked them to keep their silence? I assume you asked them to wait for you to make your own announcement."

"I did ask before they left. Nina won't say a word and no one will guess from her behavior. But Alex? Even if he keeps his silence, I'm not so sure he can hold back his emotions. He's mad—which I think is ridiculous because I'm a consenting adult. I am damn tired of this family treating me like a flighty nitwit who doesn't know her own mind. So it's going to be time to tell them soon."

"They're your family," he said, his hand resting on his Stetson beside him as if he took comfort from it the way she did her cat. "You have my support in however you decide to handle the announcement. I do want to be there with you."

"Okay, I'm all right with that. I think we need to tell them about the baby after the final event in Fort Worth. We can say we're still working out the details between us, but that we're committed to doing the best by our child."

"You can say that and I'll support you. That doesn't mean I agree with you." He leaned forward, elbows on his knees, eyes skimming her turquoise and gold–trimmed maxidress, taking in every inch of her as he always did. "I want to marry you. I would like them to know that."

"No, absolutely not." She shook her head adamantly, remembering the way he'd looked at his ex. The shine in his eyes and warm quality of his face as they slipped into easy conversation. That, more than anything, had assured her she was making the right decision. She would not rush into this and wind up with only a shell of a man doing his duty. "They'll all pressure me to say yes and I can't take all of them coming at me that way."

He frowned.

"What?" Did he know she was withholding her deeper concerns?

"If they say so much as a cross word to you, I'm going to have trouble with that. I don't relish the notion of all of them coming swinging at me, but I'll handle it."

The thought of another fight breaking out made her shiver. A follow-up thought popped to mind. "Is that why you proposed? Because you care what they think?"

"Hell, no, and frankly I'm offended you think that of me." He held her eyes with unwavering intensity. "I proposed because I want us to be a family. I want us to bring up the baby together, no split-time parenting."

Something she wanted, too. But was that enough to build a marriage on?

"And if it doesn't work out between us and things turn acrimonious?"

"It will work out. I care about you, Amie." He said it so earnestly she wanted to believe he meant more than that. "I won't fail again."

He wouldn't fail? Like they were a work project? The thought sent her spiraling. His honor and protectiveness weren't in question. But she wanted more from him than just "caring" about her. She wanted… Her heart lurched as if the plane had lost altitude, realization making her unsteady.

She loved him. She loved Preston Armstrong. And she wanted him to propose because he loved her, too.

Preston was losing control fast. Something had shifted with Amie during their discussion on the flight. She'd shut down and clammed up. He'd seen this volatile woman go through many emotions, but closed off? That was never one of them. Even when she was icy, it was that cold ice that burned. This shutdown came from buried emotions. She'd left the plane as quickly as possible, abandoning her luggage except for her cat. She'd even taken the waiting limo and said she needed to leave immediately, mumbling an excuse about needing to get a vial for the cat.

He didn't know what he'd done to flip things so fast other than asking to marry her, for heaven's sake. He'd even told her he cared about her, as Dara had reminded him to say. And it hadn't made things better. In fact, they were worse off than before, and he wasn't sure what move to make next.

He'd caught a ride from one of the flight-line crew back to the ranch to find her. She wasn't answering her phone. He got out to the ranch, a buzz of activity with vacationers taking riding lessons and the kids' camp off to the side. The resort side of the main lodge was busy, as well, but the private living quarters looked quiet.

He saw the limo backing up beside the barn, attempting to turn around to leave. He jogged over and knocked on the chauffeur's window.

The electric window slid down. "Yes, Mr. Armstrong? I was just coming back to pick you up. Miss McNair said you were conferring with the pilot."

"I found my way back. Thanks. Which way did Miss McNair go?"

"She handed the cat to one of the staffers and headed to the barn. She said she needed to ride Crystal to clear the cobwebs."

Riding? Pregnant? Was that wise? Panic rolled in his gut.

"Thank you for the information," Preston said, already jogging toward the main barn. He readied his personal sorrel quarter horse, Chance, waving aside the stable hand that offered to help. Leather creaking, he swung up into the saddle. He looked down at the stable hand. "Which way did Amie ride off?"

The employee pointed toward the forest to the east, away from the kids' camp. Off to privacy and away from the more beaten trails. Preston urged Chance forward. The horse leaped instinctively, digging hooves into earth with as much desperation as Preston felt. He set off after her, unsure what he would say when he found her but knowing he couldn't leave things this way.

The wind whistled in his ear as his horse galloped. He gave Chance his head, pressing his legs into the horse's sides. He needed to find her. Quickly. While the speed was safe for him, it made him afraid to think of Amie racing over trees and creeks—afraid for their child and for her.

Finally—thank God—finally, he saw her in the distance, her dark brown hair streaming behind her as she took the trail with her white Arabian.

She sat deep in her seat, a saddle of black and silver with a bridle to match. She looked like something out of some Western fairy tale. Her long dress flowed and rippled, hints of bare leg flashing above her turquoise cowboy boots. She was intriguing. Gorgeous. Wild and untamable. Infuriating.

Irresistible.

He galloped alongside, shouting, "Amie, slow down. Let's talk."

"Let's ride," she shouted back, hair whipping across her face.

Crystal's pace opened up and the space between them doubled. Tripled. Her grace, even here, was perfect. The way her arm fell casually to her side. She moved in perfect time to the mare's beat.

God, how he wanted to take her up on that offer and just let loose on their horses, riding the expanse of the land. But he had to be careful, for her sake.

He pushed Chance onward, making sure he was close enough to be heard. "Are you sure this is safe for you and the baby?"

Her face creased and she didn't stop, but she slowed to a trot. She sat perfectly balanced, reins gathered in one hand as she swiveled to face him. "You know, pregnant women ride horses, drive cars and even go swimming. It's quite the revolution."

"I'm not laughing." He eased his quarter horse to a trot in step with hers and reached to take her reins.

Her eyes flashed with fury at his taking the lead. "Duly noted and not surprising."

"Please, get off the horse," he said through clenched teeth.

"I wouldn't risk my child," she snapped.

"*Our* child," he snapped back, slowing Chance to a halt.

"Walking up the stairs is more dangerous than riding this horse." Still, she slid off Crystal's back, her boot thudding the ground beside his.

"Then I guess you'll be taking the elevator."

"Are you one of those smothering kinds?" Her chin jutted, challenge in her eyes as she took her horse's reins back. She stroked the Arabian's arched neck and clucked softly to her. Crystal sprung to attention as Amie guided her around Preston.

"I'm one of those careful kinds. It's how I've become such a successful businessman. Why would I take more care with work than with my personal life? I'm learning about balancing that."

"Good point. If it makes you more comfortable, I won't ride again once I return my horse to the stable." She withdrew from him again.

Shutting down.

"What's wrong?" he probed, dropping his horse's reins, effectively ground tying the well-trained mount.

"Nothing." She tightened her grip on the polished leather of her horse's reins, not slowing down. Continuing away from him, to the forest line.

"Damn it, Amie, you're upset about something."

"We don't know each other well enough for you to read my emotions." She stopped. Turned.

"Are we going back to that again? Fine, I won't press for marriage. We'll go back to dating."

"I'm not some fragile flower." She dropped the reins at her feet, leaving Crystal as she stomped toward him. "I'm not an airheaded person who's too stupid to live. Treat me like an equal, damn it."

He didn't have a clue what she meant. Why she was so angry. Or what the hell had gotten under her skin. But he knew a spark when he saw it, and she was sparking all over him.

"Treat you like an equal?" He fought for calm. Control. Couldn't seem to find any as he dragged in a harsh breath. "Remember—you asked me to."

Her brows furrowed for all of an instant before she seemed to guess his sensual intent. He angled toward her.

But she beat him to it, lunging closer to fling her arms around his neck and damn near kiss his socks off.

His brain raised a protest for about a fraction of a second—shouldn't they be talking?—before his body got fully on board with this plan.

He wanted this. Needed this.

Lifting her off her feet, he backed her up against the trunk of a massive bald cypress tree, hiding her from view, even though they were far from the ranch and not close to any trails. Her hands already worked the buttons of his shirt, her lips dipping to follow where her fingers had been. He reached to skim a hand under her hem, letting the dress bunch around her thighs while he cupped a palm between her legs.

Her head fell back, eyes closed, lips parted. She was so responsive. So hot and ready for him. Despite everything that didn't work for them, this did. The electric connection that torched away anything else.

With one hand he palmed her thigh, lifting her leg to wrap around his waist and giving himself better access. With his other hand, he slipped beneath her panties to stroke her until she went breathless, her fingernails catching on his back as she held herself still for his touch.

She amped him up so much. Unfastening the fly of his denim, he shoved aside her underwear just enough to take her. The thin strip of lace gave way anyhow, leaving her naked as he sank deeper inside her.

His groan mingled with her soft whimper, the pleasure undeniable. He cupped her cheek with one hand and slid a palm behind her back, making sure not to press her into the tree bark. She didn't seem to notice, though, her hands stroking through his hair and down his back. She kissed his chest and breathed along his skin, warming his flesh, driving him out of his mind with her sweet, sexy ways.

A breeze rose, scattering a few old leaves around his feet and plastering his shirt to his back. Amie's hair lifted, blowing around him, too. She tipped her head back as if she enjoyed the feel of it. The wildness of it. He edged a shoulder sideways a little so he didn't block her from the brunt of it, letting her feel the force of it on her face.

Her eyes popped open then, blue gaze meeting his

for one fierce, unguarded moment, and she smiled at him in a way that dazzled the hell out of him. Made him want her more. Forever.

Fueled by frenzy and too much emotion, he thrust into her again. And again.

"Preston!" She called his name in a hoarse rush right before she found her release, her body convulsing around him in the soft clench of feminine muscles.

He followed her a moment later, his own fulfillment slamming through him. His heart pounded hard against his chest, their bodies sealed together while they twitched through aftershocks of a passion bigger than the Texas sky.

When she went still against him, he could almost feel the taut strain creeping into her shoulders and back. Just like that first time they'd been together, the aftermath went tense as she relegated him to a place outside her life. He settled her on her own feet.

His head rested in the crook of her neck, his breath coming in pants as he struggled to get his galloping heartbeat under control. "Amie, you're tearing me apart here."

He remembered that moment of connection when the wind had kicked up. He hadn't imagined that.

Yet now, her hands smoothed along his hair, over his shoulders, but her eyes were distant. "I'm sorry, Preston, I'm so sorry." A sigh shuddered through her. "I just think this is all too much too fast. We should keep our distance until we figure out a plan. It's the only way to stay objective."

A cold lump settled in his gut as he angled back. "Are you dumping me?"

She smoothed her dress into place, not meeting his gaze. "I'm protecting us and our child from heartbreak."

Too damn stunned to know what to say. It wasn't often he'd been struck speechless, but right now was one of those times. He could only stare at her as she moved away from him, talking softly to Crystal as she approached her horse and then stroked the animal's muzzle.

She swung up on her horse again. She didn't race off, giving him time to make the trip with her. She kept the pace at a slow trot, but she didn't look at him or speak again all the way to the stable. Once they returned, she slid off her horse, handed the reins to a stable hand and walked away.

Her silence and stiff spine spoke louder than words. Preston waved off the stable hand, insisting on untacking Chance on his own. He needed time to think. Spending time in the barn was more productive then locking himself up indoors.

Inhaling the smell of sweat and hay, Preston attached his horse to the crossties. He loosened the girth, gave Chance a pat on the shoulder and heaved the saddle off. The sorrel shuddered from withers to tailbone as his saddle was removed.

Preston dutifully brushed and hosed the horse down. Once again, he found himself escaping in a rhythm of routine. Avoiding ghosts.

His window of time to win her over had closed unless he came up with a Hail Mary fast. A way to break through her insecurities and let her know how much she meant to him. How much he cared.

Cared?

With a sinking sensation in his chest, he knew that

was far too tame to describe the way he felt right now. Her rejection gutted him after lovemaking that had been one of the most incredible experiences of his life. After a week of witnessing her talent, her generosity and her warmhearted ways up close.

"Cared" was the cop-out of a man too scared to face his own ghosts. But he was ready to do battle now. Because he knew that he felt a whole lot more than that for Amie.

He loved that woman. Heart, body and soul.

Twelve

Amie had never felt less in the mood for a party.

But this final wrap-up of the Diamonds in the Rough promotional tour was crucial to finishing off her deal with her grandmother. And beyond any "deal," she wanted Gran to be happy. This would likely be her last celebration, a fact that tore at Amie's already raw emotions.

Preston's overprotectiveness, his anger, then his tender lovemaking had been every bit as much of a roller coaster of feelings as her own. What were they doing to each other? How could love be so damn complicated?

She stepped into the largest barn, an open space used for entertaining, the same location her cousin had used for his wedding just a week ago. Rustic elegance. The signature of Diamonds in the Rough.

Bales of hay and leather saddles made eclectic showcases for high-end jewelry with pricey stones and intricate carvings. And not just women's jewelry but men's as well, along with belt buckles and boots. Light from the chandeliers refracted off the jewels, sending sparkles glistening throughout the room and over the guests. The room was bathed in splintered, glittering light. All the indications of a lovely evening. One she couldn't enjoy.

Amie had reached into the back of her closet for a gown, barely registering what she wore. Somehow, she'd ended up in one of her old pageant gowns. A black strapless number, fitted at the top with a floor-length, poofy tulle skirt studded with tiny diamonds and silver flecks. She'd always felt like the bad Disney princess in this gown. And it was too darn tight across the chest now, thanks to her pregnancy breasts. Her cleavage was getting more attention from some men than the jewels.

She just had to get through the evening without crying over the mess she'd made of things with Preston. And then she saw him across the room, looking as sexy and brooding as ever in a black tux with a bolo tie and Stetson, cowboy boots polished. He looked so...

How could she love him so much and still have so many doubts?

Her stomach rumbled and she realized she'd been so upset she'd forgotten to eat. She turned toward the buffet, only to stop short. Her parents were standing there. On a good day, dealing with them was taxing. But tonight? Tonight they threatened to send her nerves out of control. Undo what little stability she had.

She and her brother had always thought her mother's collagen-puffy lips and cheek implants had changed her appearance until she looked like a distant-relative version of herself. Not her mother, yet eerily familiar. Her father always worked to look like an efficient business-man. Ironic as hell, since Garnet McNair carried an in-name-only title with the company, some kind of director of overseas relations. Which just meant he could pre-tend he worked as he traveled the world. Mariah only requested that he wine and dine possible contacts and charm them. On the company credit card, of course. Her parents were masters at wringing money out of Gran. But they would have to learn to live within their trust-fund means soon enough.

Her eyes burned with tears at the thought and she turned away fast, searching for Gran. She found her grandmother in the back of the room, away from the noise, sitting in her wheelchair, holding court with dif-ferent loyal business contacts.

Amie angled through the crowd, smiling and nod-ding, her full-skirted gown brushing tables, chairs and people on her way past. As she neared, Gran ended her conversation with two jewel suppliers and turned her attention to Amie.

Gran patted the chair next to her. "Your business trip seems to have been a success."

"We completed the events." She smoothed the back of her dress and sat in a cloud of black tulle. Her hair was swept back on one side with a large pewter-and-diamond comb, leaving half the silky mass to fall over her shoulder.

"So you believe you and Preston can work together? You can accept him as the CEO of Diamonds in the Rough?"

It would be so easy to just say yes. Instead, she found

herself asking, "Gran, why didn't you ever ask me if I wanted to be considered for the job?"

"Did you want the job?"

"God, no," she answered quickly, surprising even herself. "I believe I could do it, but I'm like Gramps. I'm the artist. I just wanted to be considered. To be asked."

Her grandmother took her hand and squeezed, her grip still firm in spite of her thin frailty. "I know you could have handled the job, but I also knew you wouldn't want it. I assumed you understood that. You are my amazing girl, everything I could have hoped for as the next matriarch to lead the family. *The family.* You know that's much more important than the company. You are the McNair glue that's going to keep our empire cohesive—Diamonds in the Rough, Hidden Gem Ranch and HorsePower Cowkid Camp."

Her grandmother's words surprised—and touched—her. "You really think so?" Amie's own words came out in a half whisper.

"I do." She nodded with confidence. "And if you feel the artist well is drying up and you need a change of pace, I can also see you on the board of directors, even leading the table someday. You're a force to be reckoned with, my girl."

Tears welled in her eyes that had nothing to do with hormones and everything to do with a lifetime bond she felt to this woman who'd been the true mother figure in her life.

She leaned in to hug her grandmother. "I love you, Gran."

Her grandmother wrapped her in a hug, the familiar scent of gardenias enveloping her with memories. "I love you, too, Amie dear."

Amie held on tighter, her voice choking. "I'm going to miss you so very much."

"I know, sweetie." Gran pulled back, brushing the two fat teardrops from Amie's cheeks. "And I'm sorry we didn't have more time together. But I am at peace about all of you and the legacy your grandfather and I built. I miss him. We're going to have a beautiful reunion in heaven, he and I."

Amie smiled, wobbly but heartfelt. "Say hello to him for me."

"I will." She touched Amie's stomach lightly. "If it's a girl, will you name her for me?"

Amie blinked in surprise. "You know?"

"I suspected, yes, and I am assuming Preston is the father." She narrowed her gaze. "I didn't miss the quick exit you two made for a certain coat closet that first night."

Oh, but those eyes had always seen so much, hadn't they?

Amie could only nod slowly, her eyes darting to Preston then back to her grandmother. "Is that why you sent me on the trip?"

"I didn't know then, actually, just knew there was something between you and Preston. I guessed about the baby when you got back."

"How?" She had to know what gave them away.

"He treats you like spun glass."

Amie winced. Now, wasn't that a sore subject? "I don't want him to be with me because of the baby or the business."

"Good Lord, Amie, have you looked in that man's eyes when he's watching you? He's been in love with you since day one."

Amie shook her head, wanting to believe but still too scared to hope. "You're just seeing what you want to see."

Her grandmother took her face in her cool hands. "You're afraid to see what's really there. But take a look. Take a risk. The payoff is beyond anything you can imagine. Watch with your heart rather than your eyes." Her voice softened and she cut off any chance of response as the chandeliers dimmed. A spotlight illuminated the dais where the band finished their song and Preston stepped up to the microphone.

Amie's throat burned as she looked at him. And wished.

"Thank you, everyone, for joining us here this evening." His voice still made her nerve endings twitch to life, just like that first night when they'd met. "For those of you who may not know my face, I'm Preston Armstrong, the CEO of Diamonds in the Rough. I'm also known as the interloper brought into a tight-knit family business."

He paused as laughter rippled through the room. Once the silence settled again, he continued, "I'm a man of numbers, a businessman, but in my soul I appreciate the beauty of art my skill set could never create. However, it is my honor to use my experience in the business world to bring that beauty into the lives of others."

That's what she wanted, too. She found herself nodding, embracing his company philosophy in a way she hadn't allowed herself to before. She'd been so busy avoiding him, she truly hadn't let herself hear the good things he was doing for the business.

"And on that note," he continued, gesturing toward a

screen that immediately illuminated. "The art speaks so much better than I ever could. So I'll turn over the stage now for our presentation of Diamonds in the Rough's most popular brands—as well as unveiling an exclusive first look at a new line in development by our top designer, Amie McNair. It is our hope that this new direction will add a division to the company that will bring new jobs into our community." His gaze found hers in the audience. Warmth radiated from his eyes. "And now, if you'll all turn your eyes to the screen, I give you... the heart and lifeblood of Diamonds in the Rough."

Fingers sliding into her grandmother's hand, Amie's heart leaped into her throat at his words.

The film presentation held so many of her designs, even Amie hadn't realized until then just how large her stylistic imprint had been on the company. Guests oohed and aahed as audibly as they had over the fireworks at Stone and Johanna's wedding, the jewelry brought to life with cinematic flair.

And then the screen scrolled an announcement for the future, images from her sketchbook fading in and out, the snake-themed coils she'd designed, the patterns of their markings inspiring interlocking pieces for multicolored chains in precious metal. They were more urban and sophisticated than the rustic-luxury items that were the company cornerstone, potential crossover items for a younger, more international market, while staying true to her roots.

This was the new program he'd spoken of. The new division that could create jobs and bring some of their former employees back. Realizing how well this man knew her—how well he had listened—made her heart swell. Truly listened to her wishes, her choices, even her style. He let her be—herself. Something she didn't take for granted after the way she'd grown up. He didn't stuff her into a category.

He accepted her. Flaws and all. And she owed him the same acceptance. She needed to take her grandmother's advice and be brave, take the future waiting for her.

Shining right before her eyes.

Preston sat on a bale of hay on the stage, the barn quiet in the aftermath of the final stop on their gala tour. A success in attendance, and the feedback on his presentation had been unanimously positive from the board of directors.

But there was still one person left to hear from, the opinion that mattered most.

Amie's.

As if conjured from his thoughts, she walked into the empty barn, weaving around the tables and chairs that would be cleared away in the morning. She was a vision, wearing her version of a "little black dress." So very Amie. She was one of a kind and he wouldn't have her any other way. He needed to tell her that, in no uncertain terms, to let her know he loved her. No more running. No more cop-outs. No more ghosts. She was worth every risk. Had always been worth the risks.

Her dress swished as she walked. "Thank you."

"For what?"

She stopped in front of him, her gown brushing his knees, blue eyes shining. "For the presentation. For your faith in my work. For loving me."

Her pronouncement stunned him. How did she…? Hell, he wasn't sure what to think. He slid off the stage and stood in front of her. "You know that? I was about to tell you and you've preempted my speech. But you trust that I do love you, right? I have since the first time I saw you. I can't explain it, but I do." He gathered her into his arms and held her close, something he'd feared he might never get to do again.

She tucked closer against his chest. "It would have helped if you'd told me sooner."

"My ex-wife said something a lot like that," he muttered under his breath.

She angled back to look up at him. "You talked to your ex about me?" She waved and shook her head. "Never mind. That doesn't matter. Why didn't you listen to her?"

"I guess I'm thickheaded."

"But not unteachable. The McNairs are strong-willed people, too. We can be difficult, but we are so worth the effort." Her smile was brighter than diamonds.

He cupped her waist and lifted her to sit on one of the saddles that had been used to display studded reins.

"Amie, I want you to marry me. This is about you. Nothing and no one else. You've turned my life upside down from the moment we met. I haven't been able to stop thinking about you, and yes, wanting you. But for so many more reasons than the fact that you're hot as hell. You're smart and strong. You're loyal and loving. I need that—I need you—in my life. Please make me the happiest man alive and say we can spend the rest of our lives together."

She tugged him close until they were face-to-face, close enough to kiss. "I want nothing more than to marry you. I've fallen crazy, impulsively, in love with you. No matter how hard I've tried to fight it, I can't help myself."

He listened to her, hardly daring to believe how fortunate he'd been to find her. To win her.

"I can't help myself, either." He traced the line of her jaw. The soft fullness of her lips. "I've built a reputation on being the most controlled person in the room, the CEO with the cool head, and yet you took one look at me and undid all that without saying a word."

Angling his lips over hers, he brushed a kiss along her mouth. A tender, forever kind of kiss.

He gathered her in his arms, trailing hands across her silky bare shoulders. Through the soft fall of dark hair that blanketed one arm. He breathed her in, her scent imprinted on his brain the way the feel of her had imprinted itself on his body.

Deepening the kiss, he stroked along her lower lip, demanding entrance she was only too willing to give, her whole body sighing into his as the tension left muscles at last. He kissed and kissed her, not caring about anything else but this moment with her. They might have forever, but he wanted to savor every moment with her, not taking any of this for granted.

He pulled her hips to his, knowing his whole world was in his arms. In her. He was a lucky, lucky man.

Ending the kiss with a final nip on her bottom lip. "Mind telling me why you fought something this amazing?"

"You know why," she said, her blue eyes swimming with emotion. "The fear of losing love is scary."

Of course. The answer was so simple and so complex at the same time. He'd fought against those same fears. "I can't promise a perfect, trouble-free future.

But I can promise you'll never have to doubt me or my love for you."

"You're a man of your word."

"That I am. And I look forward to proving that every day."

Epilogue

Nine months later

Amie smiled with pride as her husband thanked the family for attending the outdoor baptism held at their private new spread on the Hidden Gem Ranch property. Their home—having built a house of their own on five acres, away from the resort activity.

Preston stood with her in the landscaped gardens full of multicolored flowers, their own private jewel box of petals. He spoke to their guests as they stood together under a bower of roses holding their twins. "Amie and I can't thank you enough for joining us in celebrating the joy of our two precious—vocal—bundles of joy, Mariah Armstrong and McNair Armstrong."

He paused for the laughter before continuing the speech he'd spent more time preparing for than any boardroom presentation. He was excited—and so proud. She'd never known she could be so exhausted and happy all at once. She took her squawking son from Preston, while her husband held their daughter and kept speaking to their families—hers and his. His parents were regulars now, flying up for visits.

Amie inhaled the sweet scent of baby shampoo, McNair's unbelievably soft cheek pressed to hers. Perfection.

She should have considered she might be pregnant with twins, given she was a twin herself, but she'd still been stunned when the doctor picked up two heartbeats and then the ultrasound showed two babies. Her pregnancy had been blessedly uneventful. She'd even made it to thirty-eight weeks pregnant, giving birth to a seven-pound daughter and six-pound son.

Alex had joked she'd always been an over-the-top kind of person. Preston had just smiled, declaring her and the babies perfect.

As much as she'd missed her grandmother that day, she could feel her spirit smiling down in happiness. She felt that feeling even now, all around them, celebrating the family. With the sun shining on their happy haven, their family and closest friends beside them to help them celebrate, Amie had never felt more blessed. Family truly was everything.

She smiled up at Preston as he talked about the joys of second chances, expressing his gratitude for being a part of their family. She snuggled McNair closer, her heart overflowing with love for her babies. Their babies.

Johanna and Stone had adopted a toddler daughter six months ago and since seeing the babies, their little girl was already asking for a sibling. Alex and Nina had married last month, and Cody was already calling her Aunt Amie. He was a McNair in all the ways that counted. He had taken his job of watching over Roscoe the cat very seriously today, and Amie was pretty sure Roscoe the cat took his job watching over Cody darn seriously, too.

The cat twined around the boy's feet where they played together in the rock garden between the lilies of the valley and the gardenias.

And what a treat to have their house complete in time for the baptism. The three-story stucco home had airy porches and large rooms with plenty of space for the children to play while she and Preston watched in awe. She couldn't imagine the awe would ever go away.

She worked on designs from home three days a week, and Preston had installed an office for himself in their house to spend more time with his family. They were making it work, being with their children and keeping the McNair legacy alive. She wasn't sure she was ready to call herself a matriarch any time too soon, the way Gran had mentioned, but then again, it felt right to host all of her and his family here, under her roof. She had large shoes to fill, but she would enjoy trying.

Her parents might not have given her the upbringing she'd hoped for, but they seemed to be embracing the grandparent role with Alex's stepson and now with little Mariah and McNair. They'd come today and so far had been pleasant—maybe they'd all learned the importance of family and acceptance after losing Gran.

Preston wrapped up his speech and waved for everyone to help themselves to the brunch buffet by the pool. The beautiful chaos commenced. Preston kissed her cheek before stepping away to speak with his parents.

Alex stepped beside her, sliding a brotherly arm around her shoulder. "Gran would love all these kids playing on the lawn."

Amie could swear she smelled her grandmother's gardenia cologne on the breeze. "A familiar sight, that's for sure."

Their cousin Stone joined them, the three as close as siblings, having grown up under Mariah's care. "Our parents all seem to be better at grandparenting than taking care of their own children. I can live with that."

"True," Amie agreed. "Gran would be happy about that, too."

Stone nodded to her husband. "Preston's working out well on a lot of levels." High praise from the former CEO of Diamonds in the Rough. "You look happy. And the company's in capable hands."

Alex shook his head wryly. "Funny how that all worked out. Hell, I even like the guy."

Amie grinned up at her brother and cousin. "Love you guys."

They both tugged her ponytail at the same time.

Alex said, "Love you, diva."

Stone said, "Love you, brat."

And the teasing didn't bother her in the least. She heard the affection. They both rejoined their wives as Preston brought Mariah over, one tiny foot peeking out of a pink lightweight blanket.

"Everything okay?" he asked.

"Absolutely perfect." She leaned back against his shoulder and kissed her daughter's foot before tucking it back under the blanket. She felt the studious weight of his gaze and looked up to find his eyes serious. "What?"

"You've made me happier than I ever thought I could be. I hope you know that."

"I do," she promised. And meant it. "That's a very reciprocal feeling. Do we still have a date later tonight after the babies are asleep and the nanny can watch over them?"

"Yes, ma'am, we do." He skimmed a kiss over her lips. "I have a surprise cooked up for you, something to do with a nighttime picnic in the backyard, complete with a private showing of a Wild West film on an out-door screen. I might have even arranged for someone's favorite pizza in all the world to be specially flown in for the occasion."

Amie laughed, remembering their perfect date in Central Park. "You wouldn't be so extravagant."

"Possibly just this once." He brushed a kiss along her lips. "I'm still in the honeymoon phase of this marriage, Amie. You're going to have to excuse my indulgent side."

Her heart warmed that he took so much time to think about what she liked.

The rest of the party fell away—even with family and babies and a senior cat at their feet.

"I think I can make special accommodations for you," she whispered, gazing up into the hazel eyes that captivated her. Fascinated her. Loved her. "I wonder how long this honeymoon phase lasts."

"I have it on good authority it can last a lifetime if we're careful." He brushed a kiss on her cheek. Her nose.

"Is that so?" Happiness curled her toes as she looked out over their party. Their family. "I wonder who told you such a thing."

"Those words of wisdom came from Mariah Mc-Nair herself. She was one of the two smartest women I've ever met."

Amie's heart squeezed tight. Happy tears threatened. So she laid another kiss on McNair's head and then kissed Preston, too.

Sometimes, no words were needed.

* * * * *

If you loved Amie's romance,
pick up the other books in the
DIAMONDS IN THE ROUGH *series*
from USA TODAY *bestselling author*
Catherine Mann

ONE GOOD COWBOY
PURSUED BY THE RICH RANCHER

Available now from Harlequin Desire!

If you're on Twitter, tell us what you think of
Harlequin Desire! #harlequindesire

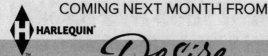

REQUEST YOUR FREE BOOKS!
2 FREE NOVELS PLUS 2 FREE GIFTS!

H HARLEQUIN®

Desire

ALWAYS POWERFUL, PASSIONATE AND PROVOCATIVE

YES! Please send me 2 FREE Harlequin® Desire novels and my 2 FREE gifts (gifts are worth about $10). After receiving them, if I don't wish to receive any more books, I can return the shipping statement marked "cancel." If I don't cancel, I will receive 6 brand-new novels every month and be billed just $4.55 per book in the U.S. or $5.24 per book in Canada. That's a savings of at least 13% off the cover price! It's quite a bargain! Shipping and handling is just 50¢ per book in the U.S. and 75¢ per book in Canada.* I understand that accepting the 2 free books and gifts places me under no obligation to buy anything. I can always return a shipment and cancel at any time. Even if I never buy another book, the two free books and gifts are mine to keep forever.

225/326 HDN GH2P

Name	(PLEASE PRINT)
Address	Apt. #
City	State/Prov.	Zip/Postal Code

Signature (if under 18, a parent or guardian must sign)

Mail to the **Reader Service**:
IN U.S.A.: P.O. Box 1867, Buffalo, NY 14240-1867
IN CANADA: P.O. Box 609, Fort Erie, Ontario L2A 5X3

Want to try two free books from another line?
Call 1-800-873-8635 or visit www.ReaderService.com.

* Terms and prices subject to change without notice. Prices do not include applicable taxes. Sales tax applicable in N.Y. Canadian residents will be charged applicable taxes. Offer not valid in Quebec. This offer is limited to one order per household. Not valid for current subscribers to Harlequin Desire books. All orders subject to credit approval. Credit or debit balances in a customer's account(s) may be offset by any other outstanding balance owed by or to the customer. Please allow 4 to 6 weeks for delivery. Offer available while quantities last.

Your Privacy—The Reader Service is committed to protecting your privacy. Our Privacy Policy is available online at www.ReaderService.com or upon request from the Reader Service.

We make a portion of our mailing list available to reputable third parties that offer products we believe may interest you. If you prefer that we not exchange your name with third parties, or if you wish to clarify or modify your communication preferences, please visit us at www.ReaderService.com/consumerschoice or write to us at Reader Service Preference Service, P.O. Box 9062, Buffalo, NY 14240-9062. Include your complete name and address.

HD15

*Brady Finn's mission is to take his company to the
next level. Aine Donovan plans to stop him. But when
searing attraction leads to a pregnancy shocker, they'll
both need to reevaluate just what it is they want from
each other...*

The door opened and there she was. He'd been prepared
for a spinsterish female, a librarian type.

This woman was a surprise.

She wore black pants and a crimson blouse with a
short black jacket over it. Her thick dark red hair fell
in heavy waves around her shoulders. She was tall and
curvy enough to make a man's mouth water. Her green
eyes, not hidden behind the glasses she'd worn in her
photo, were artfully enhanced and shone like sunlight in a
forest. And the steady, even stare she sent Brady told him
that she also had strength. Nothing hotter than a gorgeous
woman with a strong sense of self. Unexpectedly, he felt
a punch of desire that hit him harder than anything he'd
ever experienced before.

"Brady Finn?"

"That's right. Ms. Donovan?" He stood up and
waited as she crossed the room to him, her right hand
outstretched. She moved with a slow, easy grace that
made him think of silk sheets, moonlit nights and the soft
slide of skin against skin. Damn.

"It's Aine, please."

"How was your flight?" He wanted to steer the conversation into the banal so his mind would have nothing else to torment him with.

"Lovely, thanks," she said shortly and lifted her chin a notch. "Is that what we're to talk about, then? My flight? My hotel? I wonder that you care what I think. Perhaps we could speak, instead, about the fact that twice now you've not showed the slightest interest in keeping your appointments with me."

Brady sat back, surprised at her nerve. Not many employees would risk making their new boss angry. "Twice?"

"You sent a car for me at the airport and again at the hotel. I wonder why a man who takes the trouble to fly his hotel manager halfway around the world can't be bothered to cross the street to meet her in person."

When Brady had seen her photo, he'd thought *efficient, cool, dispassionate.* Now he had to revise those thoughts entirely. There was fire here, sparking in her eyes and practically humming in the air around her.

Damned if he didn't like it.

It was more than simple desire he felt now—there was respect, as well. Which meant he was in more trouble here than he would have thought.

Need to find out just how this business venture goes?
Don't miss HAVING HER BOSS'S BABY
by USA TODAY bestselling author Maureen Child

Available August 2015

www.Harlequin.com

JUST CAN'T GET ENOUGH?

Join our social communities
and talk to us online.

You will have access to the latest
news on upcoming titles and special
promotions, but most importantly,
you can talk to other fans about your
favorite Harlequin reads.

Harlequin.com/Community

Facebook.com/HarlequinBooks

Twitter.com/HarlequinBooks

Pinterest.com/HarlequinBooks

THE WORLD IS BETTER WITH

Romance

Harlequin has everything from contemporary, passionate and heartwarming to suspenseful and inspirational stories.

Whatever your mood, we have a romance just for you!

Connect with us to find your next great read, special offers and more.